Leaving
Jackson Wolf

P.A. Kane

NFB Publishing
Buffalo, New York

Printed in the United States of America

Leaving Jackson Wolf/ Kane- 1st Edition

ISBN: 978-1-7326981-6-1
Library of Congress Control Number: 2018959789

1.Kane. 2. Leaving Jackson Wolf. 3. Coming of Age. 4. Family Drama.
5. Young Adult. 6. Fiction .

Cover Design by Caroline Kane
For more information please visit www.carolinekane.net

NFB
<<<>>>
NFB Publishing/Amelia Press
119 Dorchester Road
Buffalo, New York 14213

For more information visit Nfbpublishing.com

To kids everywhere trying to find their power . . .

CHAPTER 1

McDougal had some pituitary dysfunction bullshit that made him a little runt. He wasn't the kind of runt who would cower and not fight when the bigger guys kicked him around—he just had that pituitary shit that made him little and weak. One spring day in the ninth grade as I made my way through the transition hallway, which connected the old and new buildings of South Park High School, this redheaded gorilla eleventh grader, Talty McManus, literally kicked McDougal into me. Tangled in my legs, the little shit took me down like a teetering 4 a.m. drunk, dislodging my books all over the floor. Now, I didn't really give a shit about that little runt fuck McDougal—people could kick him all they wanted as far as I was concerned—but as I lay there all twisted up with him, I got really mad at the sound of that moron gorilla McManus and his friends laughing.

Once untangled, I scooped up my heavy *Literature Today* book, jumped to my feet, and with both hands cracked McManus right upside his giant moron head. The impact caused him to stumble back into the hallway wall. His two friends were on me in a flash, and after I landed a solid right to the jaw of one of them, they locked my arms up behind my back. When he regained his equilibrium, McManus proceeded to bash the shit out of me until the shop teacher, Mr. Pierson, came and broke it up. I was still really mad and wasn't thinking about any consequences when McManus's friends let me go and I threw a punch that grazed his jaw and eventually landed on the chin of a very angry Mr. Pierson. I already had a zero-tolerance five-day suspension, and nailing Mr. Pierson would maybe get me more.

But what did I care? Five days off . . . Maybe I'd punch ten more of these morons and slide right into summer vacation.

Despite me landing that errant punch on the shop teacher, for which I apologized, Mr. Mattimore, the school principal, decided not to involve the police or any further discipline beyond the five-day suspension. Instead, the four of us—the flame-headed gorilla McManus, his two friends, and I—were sent to the detention room and McDougal, the bullied runt, was sent along to class. Mr. Franklin, the imposing security guard, babysat us as we theoretically waited for our parents to pick us up. Over the next hour or so McManus's friends were escorted out, leaving just the two of us there separated by Mr. Franklin. I settled in with a Nick Hornby book I was reading, knowing my dad, if they could even find him, would tell school officials to take a hike. I was their problem from 7:41 a.m. to 2:41 p.m.

Sitting there, McManus every so often would draw my attention away from the Hornby book and mouth the words *I'm going to kill you!* to which I responded with a sarcastic smirk and then some kisses blown in his direction from my hand. Constrained by the presence of Mr. Franklin, he was like a big dumb Irish Setter tied to a parked car, and taunting him was almost better than cracking that stupid douche upside his moron head. When he was finally called to leave, he shouted, "You're dead, Jackson!"

Yeah, whatever.

I left school later with a sense of liberation, five days' worth, and decided to walk home rather than catch the bus. I almost missed McDougal leaning up against the streetlight in front of Rite Aid in his little puke-green jacket, calling out to me in his tiny voice, "Jackson . . . Jackson."

But I just kept walking— fuck that little asshole. He didn't get the message, though, and in a voice that was probably yelling for him, said, "Thanks for helping me today."

Normally, I would've just let this pass, but there were other kids around who may have heard him, and I didn't want anybody getting the impression that I was some kind of mark for the dispossessed and runty. So I turned around, took five steps in the direction of McDougal, and said, "Listen, you little fuck, I couldn't give a shit about who kicks you around. Just don't get kicked into me. Got it?" Then, to make sure he got it, I slapped him upside the head, and the little shit crumpled to the ground like a house of cards imploding on itself.

Wincing in pain, he inched himself into a sitting position and looked up at me with his pathetic, tiny pain-filled eyes and I don't know— the better nature of myself came to the surface.

"McDougal, goddammit, get up. Stop being such a little shit." I picked his meager little ass from the ground and started to brush him off and straighten him up.

"Get off of me," he said, trying to push me away.

I stepped back and looked at him and was filled with . . . I don't know what I was filled with, but I wanted to say something, and when nothing came to me, I turned to leave.

I hadn't taken two steps when McDougal's tiny voice called out to me. "Hey, Jackson, you want to steal some beer from Rite Aid with me?"

Walking away, I called back to him, "I just got a five-day vacation. I'm not about to spend it in juvie."

Running up to me from behind with a book bag that was too big for his body, he grabbed my hoodie sleeve and said, "I know you're thinking there's cameras everywhere, but I got a way around that bullshit," and he pulled an iPhone from his jacket pocket.

Hearing McDougal curse was funny, and funnier still was seeing his disproportionately large hand gripping the iPhone. His feet also were too big for his body, but with dead seriousness, he said, "I can shut down the security cameras with this."

I looked at him skeptically, and he walked to the front of the big plate-glass windows that were covered with this week's specials on foot powder, lawn chairs, and some ginseng bullshit.

"C'mere," he said. "Watch this." And he punched some shit up on the phone and the lights blinked on and off in the store.

Impressed, I said, "Holy shit, McDougal, you're some little Jimmy Neutron nerd fuck."

"Jimmy Neutron? What is this, 2003?"

"Yeah, well, I was flipping the channels the other day . . . wait a minute, kiss my ass, McDougal," I said and slapped him on the head, but light enough so he didn't crumple to the ground like before.

He smiled up at me with teeth too big for his tiny mouth and like Elon Musk or something said, "Let's do this."

We stood there for fifteen minutes or so, waiting for all the foot traffic from school to thin out. We also had to make sure there were no customers in the store. During that time we mapped out a plan: McDougal would go in first, then draw the cashier to the back of the store where the pharmacy was located to look for some special kind of nonexistent vitamins, and when they couldn't find them, he would suggest they enlist the manager's help. Once the manager was engaged, he would jam the security cameras and then signal me by blinking the lights on and off. I would come in and lift the beer from the coolers at the front of the store.

It was all set, but as he was about to go through the front doors, unlike at school when I landed a punch on Mr. Pierson, I thought about consequences and started to get cold feet. "McDougal, you sure you can do all that?"

Looking straight at me, he twitched his fingers on the screen of the phone, and the overheads fluttered for a few seconds like a strobe light. Impressive as that was, I still wasn't completely sold and asked, "What if they won't go to the back of the store with you?"

McDougal gave me a big eye roll. Then he got up on his toes, slapped me upside my head and said with a big smile, "Normal people feel sorry for me and want to help me. They'll do whatever I ask, trust me." Walking away, he said, "Make sure you get tallboys."

And you know what, that little hobbit twit was right. It worked like a charm. The lights flicked, and I went in and could see the backs of the cashier's and the manager's heads as they moved to the rear of the store. The pharmacists were also at the back of the store, and in addition to them being very busy, their view was obstructed by rows of merchandise and advertisements, leaving the front of the store wide open. It was almost too easy. Besides a six of Rolling Rock tallboys, I grabbed some Fritos, some tortilla chips, and a tin of Altoids. Out on the street cars whizzed by, but luckily there was no foot traffic, and with a cool urgency I made my way to the side of the building.

Once there, I dispatched the Rolling Rocks from their plastic rings and barely was able to jam them into my book bag while I waited on McDougal. I had a momentary thought of ditching him, but I don't know, the little fuck had gotten to me or something. Instead, I pulled out my flip phone and sent a text to Lexi that said, *Meeet mee.* The extra *e*'s were code for her to meet me behind the closed-down fiberglass plant that was next to Okell Field.

Okell Field was at the back of both Rite Aid and South Park High School and ran the length of the buildings. On the other side of the field was the closed-down plant. During softball in gym class one day, I was looking for a foul ball in the shrubs that grew along a fence separating the field from the plant, and I noticed an opening that led to what seemed to be an ideal space to hang out.

After school I went and checked it out. There was an old steel drum that someone used to make fires, so I thought it was claimed, but I went back there a bunch of times with some of my extreme biking friends and never saw anyone. Eventually, I nipped a few plastic milk crates from 7-Eleven and made it my own. I called it "The Spot," and it was just this little space between the back of the fiberglass plant and a stockade fence that ran along the perimeter of the property and out beyond the weedy, uninhabited parking lot. There were houses on the other side of the stockade fence, but as long as you weren't crazy, you could hang back there in relative peace. After the initial runs with my extreme biking friends, I started to bring girls back there to make out. Lately, it had been Lexi.

I was growing anxious waiting on McDougal, but eventually he showed with a big grin on his face, asking, "Did you get the tall-boys?"

"Hell yes, and these too," I said, and held up the chips and the Altoids.

I turned and at a moderate pace we walked along the side of the Rite Aid and headed to The Spot. McDougal couldn't quite keep up and from behind yelled, "Is it going to be safe drinking these back at Okell?"

"I got a better place. Follow me."

Even at a moderate pace, the kid couldn't keep up. Why we needed to move like this, I didn't know. Adrenaline, I guess. But, eventually, we fell into a pace that was good for McDougal, as we talked with great excitement about how easy the whole thing had been.

Going against a stiff April breeze with dark angry clouds above us, we crossed the field, still spongy from the spring rains, negotiated the fence, and sat down facing each other on the milk crates. I set my book bag between us, unzipped it, and pulled out two tallboys. Handing one to McDougal, I asked, "Why tallboys?"

"I don't know— they look cool."

With the beers in our hands, we both hesitated till McDougal asked, "You ever drink before?"

"At a picnic I got kind of bombed once drinking from leftover cups. It was not pretty. You?"

"Just sips."

"Let's go," I said, and we lightly tapped cans. Taking a slug, we both winced in pain at the taste of the beer.

After talking about my suspension and how I was going to try to keep it from my old man, we both took another cautious drink. The bitterness of the beer lessened bit by bit with each new sip.

"I know your old man," McDougal said out of the blue.

"Poor fucking you. How?"

"Black Dogs, Outlaws. Sometimes when I spend the weekends with my dad he drags me to all those joints up and down the Avenue."

"They don't give him shit bringing you around?"

"Nah, but I don't go so much anymore, not since the accident," he said casually.

"What accident?"

"Not really an accident. I was driving my dad home from the bar and cut the wheel too hard and scraped the back end of a Chevy Cruze on his street."

"You cut the wheel too hard? . . . McDougal, you're eleven years old and three fucking feet tall. You can't drive."

"Hey, I'm fourteen and four-foot-eleven, and I can drive," he protested.

"Jesus Christ, three slugs of beer and here comes the bullshit. Maybe this drinking thing isn't going to work out for you," I said, laughing.

"No, really," he said. "My dad is kind of a drunk and a goof, and after he got a DWI he taught me to drive so he wouldn't get another one."

"Yeah, my dad is a drunk too, and the only thing I ever learned from him is how to sleep sitting up without spilling your beer. C'mon, McDougal, quit it."

"Seriously, we would pull the seat way up and I would sit on some old phone books so I could see over the dashboard, and we'd attach this contraption made out of blocks to my foot so I could reach the pedals, and then we practiced in the mall parking lot. I was pretty good. I probably got him home twenty times before I sideswiped that Cruze."

While I was in no way a scholar, I was pretty good at detecting bullshit. Sitting there looking at McDougal, with his dumb fucking Dollar Store haircut and his tiny eyes fat with excitement, I actually believed the little shit. The only thing I thought to ask was, "What the fuck is a phone book?"

He was explaining what a phone book was as pretty Lexi made her way through the opening in the fence. She sat down next to me, nodded at McDougal, and said, "Where'd you get the beer?"

"Rite Aid," I said. "It was a gangster heist." Then I pulled the tab on a beer for her and explained the day's events.

When I was done, she looked at McDougal and said, "I know you, Mr. Fundalinski's art class. He lets you use the Bluetooth, right?"

"Yeah," McDougal said. "I have sensitive ears and instead of buds he lets me listen through this." And he pulled a mini Bose Bluetooth speaker from his book bag.

Looking at me, she said, "You should hear the stuff he listens to."

Lexi had the prettiest blue eyes and the softest lips that were eternally glistening with strawberry supreme lip gloss. Being biracial, I was somewhat of a curiosity to these mostly white neighborhood girls with my blue eyes and dark skin. I had made out with a bunch of them and even felt up a few back here at The Spot, but none of them had the technique down like Lexi. Those other girls would slobber all over your face, but Lexi kept it tight and clean. Like me, she was a little messed up and didn't do so well in school, but she knew how to kiss and liked good music. No trendy stuff like Twenty One Pilots or Imagine Dragons. She liked good stuff—Silversun Pickups and Modest Mouse.

After taking her first wincing sip, she pulled a pack of Smokin' Joes menthols from her jean jacket and asked, "Got a light?"

Surprised, I said, "I didn't know you smoke."

"I don't, but my mom was being a total asshole this morning, so I stole them from her. It was her last pack. Now she's going to have to drop a ten spot on Newports at 7-Eleven to tide her over till she can get to the reservation. C'mon, give me a light?"

Neither of us had a light, but each of us took a cigarette from the pack and pretended to smoke. As the beer started to kick in, McDougal punched up some shit through Apple Music on his phone called Foxygen and then some Bon Iver. After that he went old school with "The Boy with the Arab Strap" by Belle and Sebastian. Lexi loved that song and got up and started to dance with McDougal. I guess these tunes were okay in a trendy college-radio type of way, and at first it was funny watching McDougal dance with Lexi. After a little awkwardness McDougal found some semblance of rhythm, and they looked at each other with big smiles on their faces, which made me mad. I kind of knew it was stupid to be mad and was going to get up and butt in, but instead, I took his phone and dialed up some "Slack Motherfucker" by Superchunk. They continued to dance, but the Superchunk tune was a really up, fist-waving, high-energy anthem that made you want to bounce around on your toes. Finishing my first beer and feeling a little drunk, I even got up and bounced around a bit. I followed that with some Black Rebel Motorcycle Club, "Spread Your Love," and McDougal, hearing the first heavy notes, was like, "Oh yeah, I like this."

Standing there, he fixed the unlit cigarette to his lips and started to play air guitar. Lexi took out her aviators and wrapped them over his ears. They were too big for his tiny head and he looked like a bug, a bug with a menthol hanging from his mouth playing air guitar. Lexi sat down next to me, took my hand, and put her head on my shoulder. I felt stupid for getting mad while she danced with McDougal and was on the verge of some serious self-loathing, but it was so funny watching that little runt McDougal sway and bend and do leg kicks like some badass rock star, I thankfully remained cool and upbeat.

When he was done, he sat down to our applause as we chanted, "McDougal, McDougal, McDougal." Opening the Fritos, he asked questions and searched Apple Music for more BRMC.

"I found them on Pandora like last year. Their sound isn't as heavy these days, but they're still really good," I said.

We listened to some more BRMC while we ate the chips and talked about music. McDougal, slurring a little, said he heard a lot of new music on the satellite radio station XMU and with a bit of cockiness added, "I knew about Lana Del Rey when I was seven years old."

"I love Lana Del Rey. She's like a lonesome rainy day," Lexi said.

"Eh," I chimed in, "she's okay. I mean, she's pretty funny when she talks about her pussy tasting like Pepsi-Cola, but all her songs go at the same pace, never up or down. They just sort of drone."

"I forgot to text my mom," McDougal then said in a moment of panic.

As he started to tap away with his thumbs, I took the opportunity to lean in and kiss Lexi. Even with the beer and Fritos, her shiny strawberry lips were luscious.

A minute later while I was still kissing Lexi, McDougal sarcastically said, "Yeah, don't worry about me. Just kiss away there while my mom has every cop in South Buffalo out looking for me."

"School's only been out for an hour."

"Yeah, but I have medications I take and she worries."

"What'd you tell her?" Lexi asked.

"Prince's Blade Gaming," he said while he looked up something on his phone.

"What's that?" I asked.

"It's a tabletop-gaming place. Forget that, check this out," he said, finding what he was looking for on his phone. "This is Mitski. She's my favorite."

And from the mini Bose poured a voice with that rainy-afternoon vibe similar to Lana Del Rey's, backed though by a broader range of instruments that included some ass-kicking guitar. The arrangements and Mitski's voice also had more range. Sometimes it was apathetic, sometimes it was desperate and it ticked both up and down. Whatever it was, it was really good, and you could see McDougal totally lose himself in it. We all had stuff we got lost in, but McDougal brought it to another level under that ominous gray sky when "Your Best American Girl" started to play.

Sitting there, he began to sway to her moody voice moving over a slowly picked guitar. With the additions of bass, drums, and a bed of buzzing atmospherics, the song's momentum ramped up, and the swaying turned to gentle rocking as the music permeated every molecule of his being. When the song reached its breaking point, there was an explosion of guitars, and Mitski's voice went from moody and vulnerable to a towering kind of righteousness. Jumping to his feet with a burst of energy, McDougal threw open his arms like some sort of miniature Jesus on the cross, and with his head bent upward to the sky and his eyes closed, he radiated on the spot. And with each change in the music, he contorted his little body while violently opening and closing his arms. It was fascinating to watch him become one with the tune. When it ended with these little effects, like fuzzy electric sparks being put back in a box, I turned to Lexi, wondering if she saw what I saw, and sure enough she had this awestruck, blown away look on her face.

McDougal slowly lowered himself back into a sitting position on the crate and said, "Wow, I'm really drunk."

But he wasn't drunk. Not from the beer anyway. Neither were Lexi or I. It was astonishment or something we were drunk on.

After several awkward moments of not really knowing what to say to each other, we decided to call it a day. We stashed the remaining tallboys deep in the shrub along the fence and loaded up on Altoids and walked home in relative silence. McDougal turned off at West Woodside, and I walked Lexi to her house on Tifft Street. As I made my way back to Lockwood, where I lived, it started to rain a bit, and even though I had to come up with a way to keep my five days off from my old man, I couldn't get McDougal and all that had happened today off my mind. I mean, what was that?

CHAPTER 2

I ALMOST MADE it the whole five days without the old man finding out about my suspension. The school didn't have his pay-by-the-minute flip-phone number and we didn't have a home phone, but because of a downpour, he got sent home from a roofing job and found me there sleeping instead of at school. This was Wednesday, the last day of my suspension. By that part of the week he was pretty much broke, so he was only able to stay at the bar for a few beers and wasn't soused yet. He did have a plan, though— unloading a fresh twelve-pack of Keystone *Lights* into the fridge because, ya know, besides getting shit-faced, he was worried about his figure.

Initially he was mad about how I was scamming him, getting up in the morning and then pretending to go to school. But his anger momentarily subsided—and believe me, him not angry for even a moment was a victory—when I told him how I smacked that moron gorilla McManus upside his head with my English book and how I accidently punched Mr. Pierson in the chin. Besides him not being mad for a moment, an even rarer thing occurred: he may have actually been proud of me, not only because I stood up for myself, but because I got a shot in at some elitist bullshit teacher.

But that quickly faded when I made the mistake of telling him how McManus's friends got ahold of me and locked me up. This prompted him to want to show me how to escape such a situation, but it was a stupid proposition since there was no way to recreate it with just one guy. Nevertheless, he had me lock him up with my arms under his and my chest up against his back. Going through a recent growth spurt, I was not only pushing six feet, I also was getting kind of strong, and he wasn't really able to break free of my hold. Sensing he was getting pissed, I loosened my grip and was immediately greeted by an elbow to the stomach.

All cocky, he said, "That's how ya fucking do it. Got it?"

I was really mad and, clenching my teeth, said, "Yeah, got it!"

Wearing his camouflage baseball cap, his face perpetually unshaven and prematurely lined, he looked at me skeptically for a long moment, maybe considering the need for further parental instruction. Maybe a headlock or a kick in the balls would be the right pedagogic strategy. Or maybe his tiny fucking brain was so overloaded he couldn't decide if I really "got it" or was just being a smart-ass. Life was tough when the prism through which you saw the world was limited to your angry resentments and twelve-packs of Keystone Lights.

This double trouble: anger and alcohol—was how we lost my mom. I was about six and remember them fighting all the time and my mom crying in her Creole, "So nasty, so not good . . . Why you like this?" He would tell her to shut up, maybe call her some names, remind her how he'd saved her and then go on and on about how her nigger brothers were undercutting and keeping him down. That was it, undocumented workers were keeping him from getting ahead, not his drinking or his temper.

How she ended up with him is beyond me, considering how pretty and nice she was while he was such a total asshole. I've mostly had to piece the story together myself, and best I can tell is they met when he was working on a construction crew with her undocumented brothers here in Buffalo. Their town in Haiti, Camp Perrin, got wiped out by a storm in 2002, and they had a cousin or something here. Then there was some kind of raid, and Mickey Wolf in an unlikely moment of chivalry stepped up and married my mom, who was pregnant with me at the time, thwarting her imminent deportation. I know this because during these fights he would always say, "I should've let them send you back to Haiti with your worthless brothers." And, of course, the fucking asshole endlessly repeated some variation of this to me. Things like I should be living in a hut shitting myself; I should have been earthquake food; Hurricane Matthew should have dumped my ass in the ocean. Good stuff like that.

In those early years when the old man was at work or in the bar, my mom and I had good times. She had a part-time job as an aide at St. John's Preschool, and I got to go to work with her. It was great: lots of kids, lots of things to do, and lots of fun. Also, there was Mr. Nate, a bald-headed black gentleman who ran the program and was so nice to both of us. Mr. Nate was always telling me things, teaching me special handshakes, and reading to me. He also said things to my mom that made her smile. I could tell she was trying not to smile but couldn't help herself. She was so beautiful when she was smiling, and I secretly wished for Mr. Nate to be my dad.

There were other good things too. The preschool was over by Caz Park, and we would stop on the way home and feed the ducks at the creek, collect chestnuts and play on the jungle gym. We also went to my grandmother's a lot, which I loved because she had cable and I could watch the Disney Channel and Nickelodeon.

They would sit in the kitchen and drink coffee or step outside for a smoke, mostly talking about the riddle that was my goddamn old man. I remember my mom crying and my grandmother shaking her head, saying, "His father was the same way." She was really good and sympathetic to my mom. Taught her, as best she could, all things American and always had a positive thought as we were leaving for home to face the rampage that was my old man. It was hard to believe he came from such a nice woman.

For all his bullshit, as best I can remember he only hit her once. It was a rainy Friday, and the danger in a rainy Friday was that besides the old man being sent home from work early, it was also payday. That lethal combo meant he didn't have to come home from the bar after just a few beers. And that night, when he still wasn't home at 8 p.m., my mom wrapped up the pizza we had gotten from the corner joint, Leo's, and climbed into bed with me and we read *Frog and Toad*. Nobody would ever confuse me for a scholar, but thanks to that preschool and Mr. Nate, I've always loved books and was a good reader even then. So, when the old man finally got home from the bar, he came into my room, and being little and dumb, I was like, "Daddy, want to hear me read *Frog and Toad*?"

The scent of a million beers filled my nose as he reached down, grabbed the book from my hands, and threw it against the wall, saying, "Where's my food?"

My mom got up and must have given him a look or something, because right away he was all, "Don't give me those eyes, bitch."

With my pillow over my head I fell asleep to them, mostly my father, screaming at each other. Early the next morning my mom came into my room, put on my coat and shoes, and then started to walk me out to my dad's running Ford Ranger. Holding hands, we were halfway down the driveway when the old man scooped me up from behind, smelling like a sewer, and said, "Where the fuck are you going?"

"Away from here. Give me the boy," she said, leaping at him. And as he fought her off with his free hand, I could see her eye was swollen and closed. Eventually, after she got a good chunk of his face with her nails, he set me down and grabbed her by the hair, but she broke free with a kick to his balls, and while he was momentarily doubled over cursing, she screamed and cried, "Come, Jackson. Come."

I was almost past him, but he reached out, got me by the collar, and threw me onto the ground. Screaming "I'll fucking kill you," he set after her but tripped, giving her just enough space to get in the truck and pull away.

While the old man was on the ground breathing heavily, with a trickle of blood on his cheek, she stopped a few houses down the street, got out of the truck crying, and yelled, "I'll be back for you, my sweet boy. I'll be back."

He got to his feet and tried to chase her but stumbled again and then vomited in the street as she drove away, never to come back.

After he cleaned up a bit, we walked to my grandmother's in West Seneca. The whole way there he was cursing me and my mom and yelling at me to hurry up. When we got there he told my grandmother all kinds of lies about what happened and quickly tried to leave, saying, "I gotta go find that rotten bitch." My grandmother was the only person in the world who could call him on his bullshit, and she told him, "The only one rotten here is you, Mickey. You did this, not her."

Not only did I like seeing her dress him down, but also watching him take it from her made me think that somewhere inside that asshole, there was a real human being—Severus Snape with watery, bloodshot eyes and beer breath. Rebuked, he left there with a softer stance, vowing to find my mother and make things right. But, of course, he never did, and I stayed at my grandmother's until she had a severe stroke about a year ago. We briefly tried to move her in at the house on Lockwood, but the cost of aids and therapy was too much for a hopelessly underemployed, ill-tempered drunk, and she had to go to the Erie County Home.

My grandmother was really nice and was always there when the old man would come at me with his bullshit. Even now in her debilitated state, she still had this fascinating power over him, and I never missed the weekly visit to the Home just to see him be sort of normal. I love my grandmother and appreciate all she did for me, but I don't know if I'd come every week if I didn't get to see the old man transform temporarily into a human being instead of his normal horrific self.

One week it even spilled over to the ride home. Not only did he let me change the radio from the bullshit classic rock to the alternative station, but we also shared a few laughs over a confused resident at the Home who mistook him for some guy named Larry as we were walking out. Normally I would expect the old man to tell a guy like this to kiss off, but instead he went with it.

"Larry, is that you?" said the guy.

Sticking his hand out to shake, my old man said, "Hey, buddy, how you been?"

"Do you ever see Louise anymore?" the guy asked.

"Yeah, just saw her a few weeks ago. She dropped a few pounds, looks great."

"I hear she left Sam. Is that true?"

"Yeah, that rat bastard Sam was running around on her."

"Too bad. I always liked Louise and Sam."

They went back and forth about this Louise and Sam for a while and agreed to talk next week. We laughed and laughed about it driving down Town Line Road, and when we were all laughed out but still smiling, I made the mistake of asking, "Why can't we be like this more?"

"What?" he said as the smile drained from his face.

Immediately knowing my mistake, I said, "Never mind."

"No, what? Fucking tell me."

"Never mind, it's not important." I looked out the window.

Violently, he pulled the truck to the side of the country road, and then he looked at me and asked, "Why can't we be what?"

Anything I said here was going to be wrong, so raising my voice a little, I just asked him, "Why can't we be like this . . . laughing and joking?"

The intensity on his face sharpened, his nostrils flared, and his bloodshot eyes boiled with rage, but he didn't say anything, and after a moment he put the truck in gear and pulled back onto the road. Stupidly, I thought maybe I'd gotten to him and he was contemplating what I said, but then he reached across and nailed me with a backhand to the chest. "We can't be like this because I gotta make you strong. The world is gonna kick your sorry ass so hard your fucking eyeballs are going to bleed. And I gotta make you tough enough to survive it."

He switched the radio back to the classic rock station and not only did I have to endure fucking "Kashmir" for the millionth time in my young life, but I also had to listen to him rant about how the world hates little niggers like me who aren't white or black. "Trust me," he said, "the blacks don't want you with those blue eyes, and neither do the whites."

Then he went into his usual bullshit about how I'm going to get screwed by the illegals, Obamacare, the gay agenda, lazy welfare recipients, liberal elites, Islamic terrorists, and all the rest of that Trump stuff he watches on Fox News twenty-four/seven. As far as I could tell, though, the only people who cared about the color of my skin and eyes were people his age. Kids of my generation were so past all the racial and gay stuff. I'm not saying they all liked me and I fit in, but they didn't like or not like me because of the color of my skin and eyes.

Since I mostly grew up in my grandmother's white suburban neighborhood, I guess I have Caucasian affectations. I love street hockey, extreme biking, and alternative music, and I mostly made out with white girls. There were more people of color in my old man's city neighborhood, but since moving here I didn't really connect with anyone except a few extreme-biking friends. I got shaken down by the cops a couple of times but was well schooled by my grandmother after all that Trayvon Martin and Michael Brown bullshit on how to act in such situations and had no problems. Otherwise, I kept a pretty low profile, doing a couple of Pennysaver routes on the weekend and spending weeknights at the Dudley Library at the end of my street trying to avoid the old man.

Though kids of my generation were beyond that race shit, I must admit coming from the white schools of West Seneca to South Park High School, where the races were evenly mixed, was kind of a big change. I got a fair shake in West Seneca, but it wasn't lost on me that I was different because of my skin color and my living arrangements. In the suburbs the kids had a mom and a dad. Sometimes they were together, sometimes they weren't, but both were involved. I had a grandmother and a lunatic old man, and that, more than anything, made me feel different. Now at South Park, not only was my skin color more like the general population, but so was my messed-up living situation. And instead of feeling like some oddity, at South Park I melted into the vast cultural landscape of kids who endured messed-up living arrangements just like me.

In a low-impact way, I did all right with everyone at South Park, black, white, and otherwise. At the beginning of the year I even spent some time with this black girl, Shanice Johnson. She was really cute and very forward, telling me, "I'ma get what I want." I liked her and her moxie, but she lived several neighborhoods away and came in on the bus every day, which only left us a little time to hang before and after school. I tried to take the bus to see her one Sunday afternoon, but because of shitty weekend service I either missed the transfer downtown or there wasn't one. After an hour of waiting on this phantom transfer bus, I gave up and went home. When I tried to explain what happened, she just said, "I need a motherfucker that don't make excuses." And that was the end of us.

I became friends with some black dudes in Ms. Webb's study hall too: Dontrell, Zeke, and Cordy. I was blasting some Bikini Kill in my headphones super loud one day and Ms. Webb came over, tapped me on the shoulder, and told me to turn it down. But when I took off the headphones, my head was buzzing from the volume and I couldn't process the sound of her voice. I could see what she was saying but couldn't hear her, and I must have had a confused look on my face because a moment later I could hear Dontrell saying, "That boy is brain damaged, Ms. Webb."

Everybody laughed, and walking to our next class, Cordy was like, "Man, how you listen to that Caucasian shit?"

"Nirvana dead," Dontrell said.

"It wasn't Nirvana. It was Bikini Kill," I said.

"Oh . . . *Bikini Fucking Kill*," Zeke piped in, and that was the birth of my nickname with them: *BKill.*

Mostly I sat with Lexi at lunch, but if she wasn't around I'd sit with them and they *BKill'd* me up and down. They listened to hip-hop, which I guess was all right, but the beats didn't do it for me, not like Jack White's or Sleater-Kinney's power chords. It was this difference, however, that made it possible for us to be friends in a limited way. Again, we had the issue of getting on buses going in the opposite directions, but me liking alternative music was hilarious to them and I really liked that they called me *BKill*. It all led to good trash talk.

If only the differences between me and the old man—and for that matter, Talty McManus—could bring us together. But that wasn't going to happen anytime soon, especially with that moron gorilla McManus.

CHAPTER 3

O N MY FIRST day back I was greeted by the same situation that got me suspended five days earlier. After third period, as I was walking through the transition hallway from the old building to the new building, fucking redheaded moron gorilla Talty McManus was again kicking McDougal around. Seeing me, he grabbed McDougal under the armpits and threw him into me. Though a little stunned, I was still able to sort of catch and cast McDougal aside in one fluid motion, which landed him on the floor. I stepped toward McManus, but stopped myself, thinking about the shitstorm that would come if I acted on my rage. It killed me, but I turned around and went into the new building to McManus jeering, "This ain't over, Jackson."

I looked for McDougal for the rest of the day in the halls, restrooms, and lunchroom without any luck. All day long my mind alternated between beating the shit out of McManus and that scene at The Spot where McDougal became that otherworldly travel-size Jesus listening to Mitski. Aside from a couple of direct messages on Facebook, I had no contact with McDougal during my time off. I did watch YouTube videos of Mitski and read about her on the Chromebook I bought with my Pennysaver money. Of course, we didn't have an internet connection—that would have cut into the Keystone Light budget—but in exchange for cutting her grass and keeping her driveway clear in the winter, the elderly lady next door, Mrs. Hagan, paid me a few bucks and more importantly let me tap into her Wi-Fi.

Japanese American, Mitski grew up all over the world—places like Malaysia, China, and Turkey before her family eventually settled in New York City. Biracial and never rooted to one place, she wrote songs that discussed issues of belonging and being disenfranchised. Safe to say McDougal, having been thrown through the air by a redheaded gorilla like McManus, knew firsthand what it meant to be disenfranchised. My Halfrican ass did too, and it was going to be interesting hashing out this Mitski thing with him. If I could find his little hobbit ass.

After school I looked back at The Spot, hoping he might be there, but nothing. Then I remembered that place he'd mentioned, Prince's Blade Gaming. I went home and checked the address on the internet, and it was over by where my grandmother used to live in West Seneca. I got on my BMX and headed that way.

I don't know, judging from the name, I guess I was imagining a castle or something, but Prince's Blade Gaming shared one half of a small single-story building with an accounting firm on Center Road. The entrance was at the rear, and nobody seemed to be there when I walked in. The place was dimly lit, and the walls were lined with collectible action figures, decks of cards, and board games enclosed in plastic wrapping sitting on shelves. Beneath overhead lighting there was a series of tables set up for war games with various themes, combatants, and settings that went from an arid Star Wars moonscape to an intricate Game of Thrones battlefield. I was about to leave when I heard a couple of voices coming from an opening at the back of the store. I followed the voices until I came to another smaller gaming room, and there among an array of tables was McDougal. He was sitting across from some huge unkempt kid with a scraggly beard, playing a card game. There also was an older guy, maybe mid-twenties, with the same bad facial hair and a black T-shirt that had a massive gold sword on it, watching them play. I stood there unnoticed, marveling at the stark size difference between McDougal and the guy across from him. They were playing *Magic: The Gathering*, which was one of those brainy games with a million fucking rules and strategies that I hated. McDougal, at least for the moment, hated it too.

"Got anything in that goddamn deck that isn't *Haste* or *Death Touch* creatures, Denny?" McDougal said in mock anger as he reshuffled his deck with his disproportionately sized hands.

I laughed and the three of them looked up at me, and the guy with the sword on his T-shirt said, "Hi, can I help you?"

"Hey, I was looking for McDougal."

Irritably, McDougal said, "What the fuck, Jackson? Every time you show up, I'm getting my ass kicked. Maybe it's *not* me after all. Maybe it's you."

Everybody laughed, and the older guy shuffled toward me with an outstretched hand to shake. "Hey, Jackson. I'm Mike, and that's Denny. James told us a lot about you and what's been going on at school," and raising an eyebrow, he said, "and the Rite Aid by school."

"James?"

"James . . . McDougal," Mike said.

"Oh, I only knew him as McDougal."

"That was smart of you not to go after that McManus kid today. No sense getting suspended again," Mike continued with a parental tone.

"Yeah, well, it's probably going to happen at some point," I said.

"Doesn't have to," Mike said with some calculation in his voice.

"Yeah, Denny's like the Stephen Hawking of photoshop, and he's worked up *A Brief History of McManus on Social Media*," McDougal said as Denny sort of looked away.

"Hey, Mike, my bike is outside. Mind if I bring it in?" I asked.

"Sure, go ahead."

When I came back they had a laptop opened to the photo-shopped pics of McManus. Lots of hilarious shots of him in dresses and bikinis looking so happy. Also, a bunch of really great pics of him kissing guys.

"Where'd you get all these?" I asked.

"Mostly his Facebook page," Denny said in a kind of monotone.

"We think if he's enough of a rockhead to kick James around, he's probably the type that would go nuts about photos showing him as a gay cross-dresser. I hope they don't offend you," Mike said.

"I'm not offended."

"But if these don't work and he continues to harass you or James, then we go black hole on him," Mike said, and he nodded to Denny.

Denny opened a manila folder, and there were sheets of paper containing some really nasty pics of McManus all covered in blood next to dead dogs.

"These are so bad I put them on a flash drive rather than on my hard drive," Denny said. "Hopefully we won't need them."

"So are you going to text them to him?" I asked.

"Shit can go wrong with texts," McDougal said. "We're going to print them and were hoping you could give them to him. We know where he lives."

"Why not mail them or just stuff them in his mailbox?"

"If we put them in the mailbox, his parents will probably see them first. And moms always open all the mail, even when it's not theirs. So that's no good," Mike said reasonably.

Looking at Denny, who was the size of some Jurassic Park monster, I said, "Why me? Why not him? I'm still the fucking new guy, and messing with McManus already got me suspended once. I don't need that shit."

Denny's face turned red, and he awkwardly got up from his chair and limped out of the room.

Mike went on, "Denny has some physical limitations, and should it go bad, he might have real problems." Then he raised his hand and showed me his wedding band and said, "And I'm too old and have too much responsibility to be involved in any of this."

Feeling like an asshole, I thought it over for a moment and then said, "Okay, yeah, I'll do it. Fuck McManus."

Both Mike and McDougal smiled, and then Mike exited in the same direction as Denny, leaving me there with McDougal.

Looking at him, I said, "Hey, sorry for not jumpin' in today."

"Don't worry about it. Pierson came through right after you, and I was able to get away and so did McManus," McDougal said, referring to the shop teacher, Mr. Pierson, who broke McManus and me up the day we went at it.

"Holy shit, same as last time. Déjà vu, all over again."

"I know, right," McDougal said. "Were you able to scam your old man about the suspension?"

"Almost. He found out the last day. Wasn't so bad. One elbow to the gut."

Mike and Denny came back with the doctored photos, and
a minute later we climbed into Denny's beat-up Ford Focus and
headed over to McManus's house on Harding Street near school.

Parked in front of his house, I got out of the car and went to
McManus's shabby front door and knocked. Nobody answered,
so we decided to give it some time. Waiting in the car, I found out
Denny was a seventeen-year-old junior at West High School in
West Seneca and that I vaguely knew him. All through third grade,
during morning announcements, students were asked to keep this
Denny Wroblewski and his family in our thoughts and to never
take for granted our health. I didn't know why we did this or who
this Denny Wroblewski was. Then one day at lunch a year later in
fourth grade when Denny hobbled by our table on crutches, someone said he had cancer and lost part of his leg, which explained
what Mike meant by his physical limitations.

While we waited, Denny opened up in a very understated sort
of way about the hassle of being endlessly fitted for prosthetic legs
and did a funny impression of his mom, who was sure every time
he cleared his throat or coughed it meant the cancer was back. The
smile on his face as he mimicked his worried mom made me wonder where my own mom was and if I'd ever see her again.

Sitting there, McDougal also talked about why he was so small.
He had something called hypopituitarism, which was caused by
a tumor that messed up his pituitary gland. The damaged gland
didn't produce hormones in a normal way and affected the way he
grew. With some resignation in his voice, he said he took a lot of
awful medications and hormone shots every day to help spur his
growth, but it wasn't working great.

"That's how we met, in the hospital. And Denny isn't exaggerating about his mom. Compared to her, my mom is a Zen Master."

"I get it to work for me, though."

"How?" I asked.

"Like if I pretend I'm not feeling well, she drops whatever she's doing and takes care of me."

"Like what?"

"Grilled cheese, soup, pillow and blanket, click the channels on the television," he said with a smile. He reached into his book bag and pulled out a paperback copy of *In Cold Blood*, and laughing, he said, "If I tell her I'm sick and I have to finish this by tomorrow, she'll read it out loud to me."

"No fucking way."

Both he and McDougal were nodding. "Pretty awesome, huh?"

"Does she do math?"

"She sucks at math," Denny said, laughing.

After an hour of waiting and listening to what was messed up about them and about Denny's mom, we called it a day. I took the pics and Denny reminded me that it was important to give them to McManus when his friends weren't around.

"How am I supposed to do that?" I asked.

"Maybe in the transition hallway, you pick a time and place to settle up, but first you gotta talk," McDougal offered.

"Yeah, dude is a rockhead. A redheaded fucking rockhead. Don't think he'll go for that," I said.

Seeing no good answers, Denny said, "Then how about we try this again tomorrow? You can tell us what's messed up about you, Jackson."

I laughed and said, "We'll need way more than an hour."

And with that, it was a plan.

Only it didn't quite work out that way. Next morning I missed my bus and rode my bike to school. I didn't see McManus all day, not even in the transition hall. I did see McDougal, and he said Denny was going to pick us up after school. Since I had my bike, I told him I would meet them at Prince's. I realized later, when it was too late, the smarter thing would have been to take the ride from Denny and get my bike afterward. My way, I peddled to West Seneca, got in the car, and came right back here to McManus's house on Harding Street.

But this time not thinking things through worked out for me. While unlocking my bike at the end of the day, I saw McManus get on the bus to go home and had an idea. Living so close to school, I didn't get why he would take the bus rather than just walk, other than it probably provided one last chance to terrorize some smaller, weaker freshman or something. At any rate, I realized I could just ride to his house on my bike and settle our business when he got off the bus. So I hightailed it over there, got the pics out of my book bag, and waited for him.

It must have taken all of a minute for this older lady who lived across the street from McManus to come out on her porch and ask what I was doing there . . . again? She was not convinced at all when I told her I was just waiting for my friend, and she said I should move along or she was going to call the police. Since I was a person of color in a hoodie, sort of loitering in a mostly white neighborhood, that's the last thing I needed—the police.

Not wanting to give up on this and knowing he was going to be there any minute, I slung my book bag over my shoulder and stuffed the pics into the front of my jeans and slowly went down his street, in the opposite direction of the way I would normally go home, looking over my shoulder to see if he got off the bus.

I was about twenty houses down when I saw him, so I turned around and started to peddle as fast as I could. From the way he strutted, even at a distance, you could tell he was an obnoxious jerk. Closing in, I started to get mad at the way he walked. When I pulled onto the sidewalk about two houses down, he saw me. I dropped my book bag, but still peddling hard, I went right at him, and the look of fear and confusion on his face was beyond awesome. I flew shoulder-first into him from my bike, and the impact sent both of us to the ground. Quicker than him, I was up first and was able to pin his arms to the ground with my knees, leaving an open lane to wale on his dumb Irish Setter head. But instead of pounding him, I pulled the printed pics from my pants and jammed them into his warm-up jacket really hard. I got off him and, breathing heavily in a ready stance, said, "Before we go, you fucking rockhead, you need to look at these."

He lumbered to his feet and started to come at me, saying, "You're fucking dead."

With my hands up and ready, I said, "Before we do this, just take a look at those, asshole. I had you and let you up. Just take a look, and then we can go if you want to."

Still coming at me, he casually glanced at the top one, threw them to the ground, and said, "Fuck you."

"STOP!" I yelled, extending my arm. "Look at them, asshole."

With the pics now spread out on the concrete sidewalk, he looked down. Watching him process what he was seeing was like watching Forrest Gump solve a physics equation, and when he lifted his big dumb head and looked at me, I said, "Yeah, that's you!" Watching him still not quite get it was so great, and I continued,

"Listen, if you keep fucking with McDougal and me, these and many more will hit every platform—Facebook, Twitter, Instagram, Snapchat, Reddit . . . all of them."

"Fuck you," he said, taking a half step toward me.

Still with my hands up, I had an idea. I reached into my pocket and pulled out my flip phone and with my thumb pretended to call McDougal. I didn't even know his number and may have been a little quick pretending that he answered, but I said, "McDougal, I'm here with McManus . . . You ready?" I paused another second and then said, "You decide, McManus. We go and you explain to the world why you're tonguing dudes, or we can just stop all this stupid shit."

"Fuck you," he said and took another step toward me.

"McDougal," I said, and he stopped. "Last chance, McManus."

And that was the last step he took. After another brief pause, he bent over, picked up the pics on the sidewalk, and under his breath while walking toward his house said, "Fucking nigger."

Under different circumstances I would not have taken that, but the lady from across the street was on her porch again yelling that she was called the cops. So I just picked up my book bag and laughed the whole way to Prince's. When I got there Denny, Mike, and McDougal were waiting.

"Ready?" McDougal asked.

"Not going to be necessary," I said, feeling a big-ass grin crawl across my face.

After I told them what went down, they were smiling too. I exchanged fist bumps with Denny and Mike, but that wasn't victory enough for McDougal and he jumped up to bump chests, and of course, I accidently knocked him on his skinny little hypo ass.

Didn't matter, though—he popped up and did an end-zone dance, even pretending to fake spike the ball.

When we were all laughed out at McDougal's dance, Mike took on that parental tone again. "You know, Jackson, we're glad it worked out, but the plan . . ."

In his little tin voice, McDougal cut him off. "Shut up, Mike. McManus deserved worse than getting knocked on his ass. Jackson played it just right."

In the short time I had known him, it really was kind of inspiring the way that little bastard could assert his authority in certain situations. Mike just sort of smiled and didn't say another word, the room resonating with Captain McDougal's pronouncement.

Instead of catching a ride from Denny, McDougal left with me. Part of the way he rode on my handlebars, and part of the way he walked. We talked about Mitski, and he said what he identified with was the fact there were things beyond her control that forever made her feel like an outsider. He said he felt that way and wondered if I did too?

"I don't know, I guess. But I feel it less at South Park than when I lived with my grandmother. Only problem is I have to live with my old man, and dealing with his bullshit is like a full-time job."

"That sucks."

There wasn't much else to say other than it sucked, and it sort of made me uncomfortable thinking of my feelings as they related to my old man. In my head I could hear him—*chickenshit elites* talk about their feelings and go to therapy. Real men move forward and survive.

I was happy when McDougal changed the subject to girls. He told me how much he liked Lexi and wanted to know if she had any friends.

"Friends? Yeah, she has friends."

"Friends that put out?"

"McDougal!"

"I'm just kidding," he said, laughing. "But ya know I spend my whole life with Denny and Mike. Good guys, but sad sacks. How Mike even got a girl is beyond me."

After thinking about it for a second, I said, "Well, she did say this girl Sydney Cheever had some pretty wild stories."

"Sydney? Lexi sits with her in that art class we have together. No shit, Sydney. She's so cute . . . and she's easy too? No shit," he said, clapping his hands, totally thrilled with this information.

The smile didn't leave his face the rest of the way home, but just before we reached his street, he asked some subtle questions about my BMX and my extreme-biking friends. There was something he was asking but it wasn't clear, and when I pressed him what was with all the questions, he moderated his smile and said, "No big deal. Just asking."

It was a weird ending to the day, and again as we parted ways, I was left wondering, *What's the game, McDougal?*

CHAPTER 4

As April rolled into May and the days became warmer, McDougal and I started to hang out on a consistent basis. Sometimes at Prince's with Denny and Mike, sometimes at The Spot, and lots of times at his house. Gorilla moron McManus had one last trick up his sleeve to mess with us. He and his goon-squad friends had taken to encircling us going through the transition hallway, but instead of becoming physical they would talk shit at us. To McDougal they said stuff about how easy it would be "to kill a little nerd fuck," like him and to me it was Lexi, which drove me nuts. After this happened a couple of times, McDougal broke into Facebook's HTML and embedded a single compromising pic of McManus into his newsfeed that only we could remove. We weren't hateful or anything, choosing a slinky black designer dress by Stella McCartney that really accentuated his finely sculpted ass. It was up for less than twenty-four hours, which was all the time needed to put an end to McManus's bullshit.

Another good thing with the warmer weather was the old man was back to work pretty much full-time. Usually construction work was spotty in Buffalo in the winter, and unless he got an under-the-table side job, the old man would mostly be home, subsisting on Fox News, his anger, and unemployment insurance. One day just before the weather broke, I was in the front room trying to connect to Mrs. Hagan's Wi-Fi and got his take on winter work. He was drinking beers with his mechanic friend Del in our ratty kitchen, after doing a brake job in the driveway on his latest piece-of-shit Ford Ranger. He was complaining that the construction boom in Buffalo of the past few years was making it harder and harder to collect unemployment in the winter.

And Del asked, "Why don't you just take one of those jobs?"

"Del, why the fuck would I bust my ass when for a few bucks less, I collect unemployment and stay home?" he said.

After a short pause they both started laughing and Del was like, "Yeah, fuck that."

Not wanting to absorb an elbow to the ribs or a kick to the balls, I didn't say anything, but that seemed pretty messed up. He was always bitching about not getting ahead, yet when there was all this extra work around town, he didn't take it. When he brought this "woe is me, there's no work" song and dance to my grandmother before she had the stroke, she would respond, "Mickey, that's a load of shit and you know it. All you do is bitch, complain, and blame others. You'd be a rich man if you stopped all that nonsense and just went to work."

Questioning his victimhood pissed him off more than anything, and he would storm away, slamming the door on the way out. But her getting after him never produced much of anything, either. In fact, this past winter it became my job to Google fake work leads that he would turn in at the unemployment office when he signed for his check. Otherwise, he spent the winter drinking beers, watching Fox News, and falling hopelessly in love with Donald Trump.

Trump really got the old man going. He spoke to all the resentments and grievances that so animated the old man's existence.

He loved Trump's put-downs and insults and the way he got after the liberal media. Trump appealed to and gave voice to every crass instinct that sustained his being. "Fuck Katy Tur . . . Fuck Megyn Kelly," I would hear him yell.

He was so into the election we even went to a rally during the primaries at the First Niagara Center. I was not into it at all, but he said it was important that I be involved in the political process. I guess, in his head, Trump railing against Islamic terrorists, lying Ted Cruz, and Mexican illegals was the political process.

This was such a big deal to him he got a six-pack and we tailgated beforehand. But not a bullshit Keystone Light six—this was a special occasion, so he spent an extra two bucks on Bud Lights. And sitting on the back gate of his truck listening to stupid Bon Jovi on 97 Rock, I could feel the resentment and sense of grievance in the way people looked at my blackish ass as they walked by us. And, quite frankly, it scared the shit out of me. I tried to talk him into letting me wait in the truck, but he wouldn't have it.

As a person of color who has lived his whole life in the white community, I still found it hard sometimes to read people, but what was in the hearts of those surrounding me that night at the First Niagara Center could not have been clearer. Those were twenty thousand angry white motherfuckers aiming to reassert their dominance over a culture turning black, brown, and gay. After a couple of black protesters were forcefully removed, I was feeling quite vulnerable and went into survival mode.

Truth be told, growing up with biracial Obama as president, I was kind of into politics and the election too. Sitting in the magazine section of the Dudley Library one night, I read a long, complicated article in *The Atlantic* by Jeffrey Goldberg called "The Obama

Doctrine," explaining America's change in focus away from the Middle East toward Asia, where the president made the case that Asia should be the focus of our interests in the future. I didn't know all the history, but it seemed all too reasonable. That's what I liked about Obama—he was always a reasonable steady hand. I didn't get why everybody dogged him so much. The old man said he was condescending and talked down to people like him, which I didn't get at all.

I also liked election stuff by Molly Ball in *The Atlantic* and I tried some right-wing bullshit in the *National Review*, and online I read Jamelle Bouie at *Slate*. Like most people my age, I determined Bernie Sanders was the guy who best represented my interests, but in that moment at the rally surrounded by all those ready-to-explode white people, it was a no-brainer to just submit to the mob. I cheered and chanted at every dumb thing the orange gesticulating monster at the podium said. All of it. From the thing about how we don't win anymore to chanting, "Build the wall . . . Build the wall . . . Build the wall . . ."

The next day, when I was sitting at The Spot with McDougal, telling him all this shit, he thought it was pretty messed up to tailgate and completely understood why I had to submit to the mob. We talked about other things too—music, books, hypo, his messed-up dad, more about my BMX friends—but the thing that really animated him, that filled his face with color, was talking about girls and Sydney Cheever.

It was driving him nuts knowing she was easy. Lexi said he started to stop by their table in art class, making subtle advances toward Sydney, always complimenting her and offering insight on how to improve her work: ". . . maybe you want to darken those lines" or "careful not to muddy that up." Lexi said he was so sweet and flattering, but she didn't see anything happening between them because Syd went for the bad boys, the types who would eventually be all tatted and pierced, rather than a fragile dude like McDougal.

Without a hint of embarrassment, he also told me, "Jackson, I'm killing my dick thinking about Sydney."

"Whaddya mean?" I asked.

"You know . . ." And he made the universal sign for whacking off.

"Ah . . . yeah, maybe you should direct your jacking elsewhere. Lexi said she's into dudes who get pierced and tattooed."

He got to his feet, puffed up his chest, and folded his arms, saying, "Yeah, so . . . I'm bad too. I could rock some skull-and-cross-bones tats."

"Dude, no offense, but you're like a house elf. And you ain't even a big one. You're like the Kevin Hart of house elves."

"Size ain't everything. I got game."

"No doubt you got game. Don't waste your time on someone you can't get."

"I could so mack Sydney Cheever if I got the chance."

I only knew Sydney from what Lexi said about her and from seeing her in the halls, and McDougal was delusional thinking he could get her. She was really cute with her skimpy black Metallica T-shirt, crop of burnt-red hair, and bright blue eyes outlined by a healthy dose of eyeliner. You could tell by the way she carried herself that she did not suffer foolish high school boys and that Lexi was right: she was destined to be on the back of some scar-faced, skull-tatted dude's Harley.

"You'll see," he said with conviction, and we left it there. That's one of the things that drew me to McDougal—he would never take no for an answer, and when he ran into an obstacle, he would recede with that conviction-filled, "You'll see," and quietly started to do the math in his head to solve the problem. Because of the endless shit from my old man and because I was a person of color in a mostly white neighborhood, my grandmother had taught me to think ahead about situations, but I never met anyone who thought into the future like McDougal.

After a couple of weeks of hanging out and more than a few "What was that?" moments, trying to figure out what he was up to, some things became clear about him: he was fearless, he was girl crazy, and he wanted to BMX with me. Specifically, he wanted to kick over traffic cones where construction was taking place up and down the Avenue.

The previous summer, over a span of ten or fifteen blocks, new curbs were installed along the Avenue. Where the old curbs had been extracted there were long, cavernous trenches lined with heavy-duty orange parking cones, and I and a couple of the guys, Skeezy and JuJu, riding our BMXs, started to kick the cones over, which really pissed off the construction guys. The response—chasing us, calling us names, trying to block us—only motivated us to do it more. But after our most productive outing where we kicked over like fifty cones, we were ambushed by two cop cars.

Worse than the shit they talked and worse than jail even, the cops brought me home to the old man. He nodded and shook his head reasonably while the officer explained my transgressions, but once they were gone the old man proceeded to beat the shit out of me.

That was when I first moved back in with him, shortly after the debacle of trying to care for my stroke-debilitated grandmother. He was particularly dangerous that ninety-degree day, sweating, drunk, and of course, pissed off. Yet not so much so that he wasn't still quick and agile. "You bring those fucking cops to my house . . . after all I've done for you."

I wasn't really strong enough to block the barrage of lefts and rights to my head, but when he went for his belt, that afforded me just the opening I needed to run out the door and hop on my bike and ride away as he chased me. Taking no chances, I spent the night in Mulroy Park and only came home when I was sure he was gone to work the next morning, starving and covered with a million mosquito bites. I braced myself for the worst when he got home later that day, loading up my book bag with sandwiches, water, and a thin blanket in case I had to stay at the park again, but cracking open a Keystone Light, he said, "Where'd you go so early this morning?"

"What?"

"Do I stutter? Where the fuck were you this morning, and why is your face all puffy? You weren't here when I left for work."

"Where was I? I . . . was . . . um . . ." And then it hit me. The drunken asshole didn't remember what happened and didn't know I spent the night in the park. Casually, I said, "Me, Skeezy, and JuJu went down and hit the bike park at Canalside before it opened."

Built on the long-defunct slip that once connected the Atlantic Ocean to the Great Lakes by way of the Erie Canal, Canalside was a new Buffalo hotspot that hosted all kinds of concerts, fitness classes, poetry slams, boat tours, and other stuff. There also was a bike park, and we often did go down there early in the morning before it opened to use the ramps on the down low until either the cops kicked us out or the pimple-faced attendant opened the place.

So when McDougal brought up the kicking-the-cones thing we did for a couple of weeks last summer, I was like, "How'd you know about that?"

"It was one of the weeks I stayed with my dad, and I saw you guys from Black Dog's front window. I nearly pissed my pants watching those construction guys chase you," he said, smiling.

"Yeah, well, my old man beat the shit out of me and I had to sleep in the park, so I'm going to skip the cones this summer."

"C'mon, Jackson, what're the chances of getting caught again?" he said, laughing.

"You're crazy. I'll ride with you, but not that. You have a bike?"

Of course the little hobbit bastard had a bike, and when we went to his house to check it out, it wasn't just any bike. It was a twenty-one-foot Subrosa Malum with tapered forks, Rant hubs and gearing, Shadow Valor tires, and a lightweight CrMo frame with a black pewter finish. It was freaking beautiful and really expensive.

"McDougal, this thing is phantasmic. Where'd you get the cash for this?"

"My dad and I came up with an app."

"An app?"

"Yeah, we built this little firewall thing to protect against botnet attacks."

"Botnets are digital robots that attack computers, right?"

"Right, but they don't only attack computers. There's all kinds of shit in people's houses now that connects to the web: TVs, refrigerators, microwaves, scales you use to weigh yourself, all kinds of shit. The problem with all these appliances is that the manufacturers installed very hackable hardwired passwords that make them vulnerable to botnet attacks. Some hackers launched one of these attacks and just like that a trillion toaster ovens and washing machines were trying to access the web all at once. All that incoming traffic shut down some of the big boys like Amazon and Twitter for a few hours, costing them huge jack."

"You little Jimmy Neutron fuck," I said.

"Mostly my dad, but I had an idea or two and got a cut. He's a sick engineer and would be a real player if he could put down the bottle."

"Is that why you live here instead of some mansion in the 'burbs?"

"Yeah, I guess he's forced to stay in the hood because of that. He can never stick with a job and does stuff like this on his own, but it's really spotty. My mom and I are here because her parents left her the house when they moved to Florida. It's pretty messed up at times," he said.

"Does your old man get nuts on the sauce?"

"Yes, but not like yours. He gets real chatty and starts talking about all the crazy shit going through his head. Ideas, theories, conspiracies which I sort of understand up to a point, but then it goes into the Bill Gates stratosphere and forget it. Trying to tell me all this shit is one thing, but you should see him trying to explain it to guys like your old man when he's all lubed up. They look at him like he's whacked out of his skull."

"I bet."

"Eventually, he just starts talking into his double Stoli. Mostly it's gibberish, but sometimes he has a coherent idea and if I can understand it, I might write it down. That's where the app came from—me writing shit down on cocktail napkins while he talked into his vodka."

"That's some sick shit. My old man came up with an app too. He *app*lies a left and a right to my fucking skull every chance he gets." And turning away from the bike, I punched McDougal in the arm with a left and then a right, only I hit him too hard and knocked him to the garage floor. Apologizing, I bent over to help him up, but he nailed me in the chin and bounced to his feet and began to shuffle around like a boxer with that oversized smile and that stupid Dollar Store haircut saying, "C'mon, Jackson. I ain't afraid of you."

As we circled each other, hands up, McDougal landed a few jabs and crosses to my chest, which was like being hit by one of those play Nerf bullets. Carefully, I returned fire with a couple of open-handed taps to his head, further messing up his hair.

"You better come up with an answer for this, or I'm gonna mess you up so bad Sydney will never even look at your sorry little ass."

Nailing me again, he looked at my head and said, "Abraham Lincoln called, he wants his stovepipe back," referring to my failed shark-fin haircut, which was now out of control. Normally, I clipped my own hair, usually keeping it pretty short and tight because there wasn't much cash or knowledge in this hood to meet my needs. I was good with my failed shark fin if it gave McDougal an opportunity to be hilarious, even at my expense.

"You call that a fucking haircut? It looks like a furry tornado swirling on top of your head, or maybe you're just a cheap-ass paintbrush with eyes?"

And just as McDougal was starting to really roll, a scolding voice came from the back of the garage. "James . . . language." It was McDougal's pretty mom standing in the doorway that led into the house.

Being a wiseass, I said, "Thank you, Mrs. McDougal. James was saying hurtful things to me."

"Yes, I heard," she said. "But Jackson, when are you going to get a haircut? You'd be so much more handsome if you cleaned that up." She paused for a second and then went on, "James, time for your shot. Jackson, will you be staying for dinner?"

Smiling, I looked at McDougal, and he nodded. "Um, yes. Thank you, Mrs. McDougal."

She went into the house, and trailing behind, I said, "Did you hear that? She said I was handsome."

"No, she didn't," McDougal came back strongly. "She said you'd be *more* handsome if you trimmed those pipe cleaners growing from your skull. The Elephant Man would have been *more* handsome if he got a face transplant, but in the end he'd still be the fucking Elephant Man, ya ugly piece of shit."

McDougal's mom was very pretty in a blonde Claire Danes sort of way and was a nurse practitioner. Ever since we started to hang, she took an active interest in my health and well-being. She was always looking me over, and when she found out I hadn't been to the doctor or the dentist in years, she set up some appointments at the free clinics for both. Besides checkups and teeth cleaning, I got a cavity filled and the HPV vaccine.

I wasn't used to this sort of attention, and when I asked McDougal about it, he said she was a worry wart. But, messing with him, I was like, "I think it's something else. I think she probably has a thing for young black men and wants to date me."

He protested a bit, but knew any real objections would only encourage me more and did the smart thing and laughed it off. Nevertheless, I still busted on him, telling him when I became his stepdad and was the master of the house, I was going to whip his little pervert ass every day because I knew when he wasn't masturbating, he was thinking about masturbating and he needed to be cleansed of this appalling heathen practice.

We had a great spaghetti-and-meatball dinner with salad and bread. Normally, Chef Boyardee or Spaghettios was the only way I got sauce and pasta mixed together, so this was a real treat. We didn't talk much during dinner, but on the sly I started to wink and raise my eyebrows at McDougal and then nod toward his mom. At first, he was shaking his head no. But of course, I eventually got him to laugh, to which his mom, with some irritation in her voice, said, "Boys, please eat."

After dinner we listened to some Cloud Nothings and Nada Surf through Infinity bookshelf speakers that were attached to the back wall of the garage, and we talked about girls and biking. It was supposed to rain the next couple of days, so we made plans to BMX on the weekend. Walking home later, I was really in the moment or something, feeling the breezy night air run through my hair and penetrate my jacket. It was a weird kind of feeling, and for some reason I started to think about my mom's big smile and feeding the ducks at Caz Park.

It was still only 8 p.m. when I got to my corner, and rather than face the shit at home, I crossed the street to the Dudley Library, which was open till 9 p.m. I was about to go in, but instead sat down on the bench outside the front doors and savored this good feeling that was circulating through my body. With the swirling night air and the cars rolling down the Avenue, one recurring thought kept running through my head; *McDougal, what are you doing to me?*

Chapter 5

D ESPITE THE BRIGHT morning sun, the weedy parking lot of the abandoned fiberglass plant was still wet from two days of intermittent downpours when I met McDougal on Saturday morning. He was wearing this stars-and-stripes helmet and looked totally stupid, so I took out my phone and put it to my ear, fake nodded a couple of times, and yelled to him, "Toby Keith's on the phone and wants his helmet back."

A little winded, he laughed and said, "Yeah, well tell the Tobster to suck it. It was the only one they had at Kmart, and it wouldn't fit his fat head anyway. I'm going to Amazon one later or maybe paint this one, once I figure out the kind of rider I am."

"The kind of rider you are . . . Really?"

"Yeah," he said, smiling. "Maybe some lightning bolts to show my flash. Or maybe I'll go punk rocker with a big blue mohawk."

"Before all that, how 'bout you turn those pedals over and show us what ya got."

And what he had was nothing. He was slow, unsteady, and almost instantly fatigued. It was obvious I was going to have to move at a snail's pace with him, so I started with a couple of basic stunt-peg moves. He watched, sipping a Gatorade, as I executed a stepover stance, which consisted of bringing my right foot over the back of the bike and placing it on the rear left peg while my left foot remained on the pedal in a downward position.

After falling twice, he got it, but said, "How is this going to help me to kick over those traffic cones?"

"First, we ain't kicking anything over. Second, I thought you were smart. We're doing this, ya dumb shit, because you suck and need to get comfortable on your bike."

He took another break while I added on to the stepover stance. With my right foot still on the left rear peg, I moved my left foot from the pedal to the front peg and showed him how to keep the bike going by moving the handlebars back and forth. Again, after falling a few times, once hitting his head pretty hard on the pavement, he got it.

When we moved on to wheelies and bunny hops, McDougal's lack of strength became obvious. He could sort of pull up the front of the bike for a wheelie but wasn't close to being able to bunny hop. A bunny hop is a combo move where coming out of a wheelie, you set the front of your bike down while lifting up the back at the same time, using the power of your legs and stomach. Ideally, it's supposed to be one fluid movement that looks like a hopping bunny. Lacking the strength through the middle of his body, McDougal was more like one of those old people in the television commercials who've fallen and can't get up than a hopping bunny.

After nearly hitting the pavement again, he became frustrated and said, "This sucks."

"Relax," I said. "All we need to do is muscle you up."

"How?"

"Growth hormone?" I said, smiling.

"Not funny, asshole."

Pissing him off amused me, but I kept it in check and said,

"There's all kinds of workouts on YouTube, and isn't there a dumb-bell set in your garage?"

"Yeah, my mom's Bowflex."

"Lexi is meeting me to do my Pennysaver route, and then we're going to Mighty Taco. I'll stop by after that and we'll find some workouts."

"Bring Lexi and tell Lexi to bring Sydney."

He was starting to drive me nuts with all this Sydney stuff that was never going to happen, so I said, "Forget those two. Your mom does P90X? Does she wear yoga pants?"

"Jackson," he said, smiling.

"Has she been asking about me?"

But then he turned it around. "What about your mom? She's probably hot, like Alicia Keys."

It was a pretty nothing comeback, but for some reason, I got really mad. "Listen, you little goblin fuck, don't talk about my mom."

"What?"

"Whaddya mean, what? Don't talk shit about my mom."

McDougal's tiny eyes widened with disbelief, and even though I knew I was being an asshole, I was serious and pedaled away full of anger. And as stupid as it was, my anger didn't slacken for hours and hours. I continued to quietly brood the whole time Lexi and I were doing the papers and right on through dropping the paper bags back at my house and going to Mighty Taco.

Finally, about halfway through her three-cheese nacho burrito, Lexi asked, "What's up? Why so quiet?"

I responded with some grunting sound, prompting her to say, "Fine." And with a bit of fierceness, she got up from our booth, grabbed her tray, and dumped her half-eaten burrito and Diet Coke in the garbage.

Just before she was out the door, I caught her by the elbow and said, "Wait. Sorry."

Her pretty blue eyes were fiery. "What's up, Jackson?"

"C'mon," I said, trying to guide her back to the table. "I'll get you another burrito?"

"No," she said, standing her ground. "Are you breaking up with me?"

"No. God, no. Why would you say that?"

"Oh, I don't know. For the last three hours you barely say a word to me, and when I ask you what's up, all you can do is grunt. That's why."

"No, sorry. Please, sit down. I'm just mad about some shit Mc-Dougal said to me."

"McDougal? . . . C'mon. What'd he say?"

"Just some stuff about my mom looking like Alicia Keys."

"Yeah, so? What's wrong with that?"

"Nothing."

"So why are you mad?"

"I don't know why . . . Well, I do know, at least partly. I'm mad at myself for getting mad, but I'm mad about the Alicia Keys crack too and I don't know why. It's really frustrating."

Her eyes softened and she signaled that we should sit down. Across from me in the booth again, she took my hand and said, "Does your mom look like Alicia Keys?"

"I don't know, maybe." But after thinking about it for a moment, I said, "It's been a long time, but yeah, afro Alicia Keys."

She nodded and her face brightened. "Oh, I can so see some Alicia Keys in you."

I laughed and said, "Shut up."

Gently stroking my hand, she asked, "Do you miss her?"

"Well, yeah . . . Maybe. I don't know. I mean, she was great when she was around. But where the hell is she? Why didn't she ever come back like she said she would?"

Lexi thought about that for a second and then said, "My mom can be a psycho, but she's around, and as crazy as she makes me sometimes, she does try. But my dad, I'm such an afterthought to him, and it makes me really mad."

"So what are you saying?"

She kind of shrugged. "I don't know. What am I saying?"

"That I'm mad at my mom?"

She shrugged again and said, "Think I'd be pretty angry if my mom left me with that old man of yours."

I went up to get another burrito for her and was pondering what Lexi said about how I was harboring anger for my mom. I was so lost trying to reconcile this I didn't hear the kid behind the counter until he was almost yelling, "CAN I HELP YOU?" I apologized and gave him my order, and standing there waiting, I thought Lexi might be right. Like me, I always considered my mom one of the old man's victims, and it never occurred to me to call bullshit on her for not coming back to get me.

I sat down again, and Lexi shifted gears as I set the tray with the burrito in front of her. "What's up for the rest of the day?"

I told her about the epic McDougal BMX fail and how I made plans to show him some YouTube workouts, but first I was going to have to apologize for being such an asshole to him. I also told her how he had been driving me crazy constantly talking about Sydney.

"He wanted me to bring you and for you to bring her."

This prompted a mischievous smile to spread across Lexi's face, and she pulled out her phone and started to type away.

"What are you doing?" I asked.

"Wait," she said, still smiling.

Her phone dinged and she started to laugh. "Text McDougal, tell him we'll be there in twenty. C'mon, we have to meet Sydney on the way at her corner in ten minutes."

"No way," I said, totally shocked.

But before we left, I put my hand on her arm and said, "I think you're right. I think I'm mad at my mom."

She kind of shrugged and said, "Yeah, I would be . . . It's okay," and she leaned across the table and gave me one of her strawberry supreme kisses, and I felt million times better about the whole stupid thing.

Turned out Sydney was available because she had a bad experience with some dude who was pushing her to do things that made her uncomfortable and it really scared her. So, she was taking a break from guys.

On her corner was a bar my old man frequented called Outlaws. It was probably named that way to appeal to self-proclaimed badasses like my old man. Certainly some of the patrons, like the two disheveled guys smoking outside the front door who catcalled Sydney, could be seen as badasses or bottom dwelling maggots.

Walking up to us with a muted face, Sydney nodded to me and said, "Jackson." She then turned to Lexi, who must have looked concerned, because as we started to leave she said, "Don't worry, they've been talking that shit to me since I was ten."

Though I had only seen Sydney in the halls and never really

talked to her before, between McDougal and Lexi I sort of felt like I knew her, so jokingly I said, "Want me to kick their asses?"

She gave me an appreciative little smile and said, "Next time."

The May day had grown sunny and warm in a way that communicated summer was within reach as we walked along the Avenue. Littered with bars and taverns, the Avenue was struggling to be something more in the new Buffalo. A fledgling flower shop and an optical place split a storefront, and the old Nick's Texas Hots on the corner of Choate was in the midst of a makeover. Heavy construction machinery sat quietly in an open lot, waiting to remove and replace another section of curbs this summer. Like the changing season, it felt new and positive.

Also new was the understated look Sydney was forging. Wearing high black Cons, skinny jeans, and a matching jean jacket, anchored by a black Motörhead T-shirt, she carried herself with a certain hardness. She had let the burnish fade from her red hair, and there was no eyeliner rimming her shocking blue eyes. Her only accessory was a thin strip of metal curling from the middle to the underside of her nose. This stripped-down, unplugged version of Sydney was nevertheless still very attractive.

Although I needed to make things right with McDougal, my earlier moodiness had cleared as I considered Lexi's new angle about my mom. My disposition was also helped by the mild weather and the fact I was walking down the street between these two beautiful girls. While Sydney cultivated the low-fi thing, Lexi, despite spending a couple of hours delivering papers with me, still looked more than ready for prime time with blonde highlights accenting her sandy hair, a thin strip of eyeliner ringing her dazzling blue eyes and those glistening strawberry flavored lips.

As we walked, Lexi told this creepy story about looking through a half-shaded window on McKinley while doing papers earlier and seeing this big dude in his boxers massaging a naked woman on a table.

"Gross," said Sydney. "Was he, ya know, big . . .?"

"Yeah, he was a big guy."

"No, I mean, down there, was he bi—"

But before she could finish, Lexi put up her hand and said, "I turned away before I could tell."

"Gross," repeated Sydney.

McDougal's garage was attached to his house, and a moment after I knocked on the inside door, it swung open dramatically and McDougal was standing there dressed fully in black, with a mask covering his eyes, a cape, and his bike helmet, now painted black with pointed ears fixed to opposite sides. Rasping up his tiny voice, he said, "I'm BMX Batman."

Taking in who was with me, he closed the door just as quickly as he opened it. We looked at each other, smiling, but I was the only one to laugh. McDougal was back a moment later without the Batman accessories. Smiling, he came down the two steps into the garage and nodded, saying, "Lexi, Syd . . . what's up?"

"Hey, James," they both said.

The girls were willing to give him a pass about the way he answered the door, but there was no way I could let this go. "Really, BMX Batman? What, are you going to save Big Wheels kids from marauding skateboarders?"

Everybody laughed, including McDougal, and then he said, "Shut up, Jackson."

In this situation, others, including myself, might have been embarrassed or awkward, but not McDougal. For all the things that were messed up about him, the little bastard had charisma and confidence in spades. As I looked at him beam while talking to Lexi and Syd, my skepticism about his chances of getting with her was faded fast. More and more it seemed there wasn't anything he couldn't do. No wall he couldn't knock down.

To the right of the door that led into the house was his mom's hybrid Ford Escape. While bullshitting, we unpacked some plastic Adirondack chairs and lined them up in the mouth of the garage. McDougal went inside for a moment to turn on the stereo that connected to the bookshelf Infinity speakers. Coming down the steps, he was tapping on his iPhone, and a second later some Real Estate filled the air. I rolled my eyes because I was hoping he would have played something more kicking, like Japandroids or Spoon. Or maybe take some inspiration from Sydney's T-shirt and lay down some Motörhead. But the girls, who had settled into their chairs and were sunning themselves with closed eyes, liked it.

"Who is this?" Sydney asked.

"Dream pop band from New Jersey, Real Estate."

"They're really good."

"I know, right?" Lexi added, "James finds all the best new stuff."

In a little fit of jealousy that may well have morphed into anger, I mimicked Lexi. "James finds all the best new stuff."

The girls sort of ignored my lame taunt, but McDougal was smiling that big goofy oversized smile as he sat down. Once he was settled in his seat, with the girls not looking, he flexed his muscles and then lightly thumped his chest, but instead of looking like an MMA fighter after a KO, he reminded me of a tiny Bill Nye the Science Guy, with a worse haircut, if that was possible. He was hilarious and I felt lucky to be there with those beautiful girls and to have a friend like him to share this summery day.

Though the original purpose for going to McDougal's was to come up with some workout routines, that totally got lost in the sauce with Lexi and Syd tagging along. After sitting in the chairs for a while, taking in the beautiful day, his mom came into the garage and said, "James, time for your . . . Oh, hello . . ." An awkward moment of silence ensued before McDougal's mom said, "James, you didn't tell me you had friends over. Please . . . who are these ladies? Hello, Jackson."

She smiled broadly as he introduced Sydney and Lexi. After some small talk, where it was established that Mrs. McDougal had gone to grade school with Sydney's mom, which was a weird prerequisite of every South Buffalo Irish introduction, determining how you might know each other, she asked us if we wanted snacks, which of course, we did. McDougal followed her into the house and they were gone for kind of a long time. This was about the time of day McDougal took his meds and got his afternoon shot. While we waited the three of us played a game of HORSE with an undersized basketball and a hoop on the side of the driveway.

I had both girls at HOR when McDougal came back out carrying a tray with bowls of multigrain organic nacho chips and salsa. He was trailed by his mom, who had a pitcher of iced tea and glasses. She said, "Jackson, honey, could you get me a couple of end tables from in front of the car, please?"

I hopped to it, placing the tables in front of the Adirondack chairs. McDougal set the snacks down, but his mom was *aghast* at the winter grime on the end tables and chairs and went back into the house for some wipes to clean them up. After a drink and some chips, we resumed our game with McDougal bouncing around us, reinvigorated from a fresh dose of hydrocortisone.

Cleaning the tables, McDougal's mom encouraged him to hydrate as I knocked Sydney out of the game. She went over and helped wipe down the chairs and continued to talk to Mrs. McDougal, who was beaming. I let Lexi get me to HORS before knocking her out. McDougal had settled down by then and his mom had gone back into the house. He was talking to Sydney and playing more plush dream pop by a band called Day Wave.

I was restless and talked them into a game of touch football in the street. It was boys versus girls, and in our first huddle I apologized to McDougal for being an asshole earlier.

He said, "No problem, ya little drama queen. How'd you get Sydney here?"

"Lexi texted her. Some dude messed her up and she's lying low. If you ever had a shot, this is it."

He agreed and then during that first series of plays, while running a sweep with me out in front blocking, he proceeded to throw a stiff arm, which landed perfectly on Sydney's breast, right on the *e* in Motörhead. McDougal apologized profusely and then made things worse by trying to wipe away the area he had just grabbed, thus copping a second feel. Sydney was cool about it as McDougal stammered out his apologies, even giving him a little hug and telling him not to worry about it.

Again, I couldn't just let that pass and said, "Putting the touch in touch football. Wait till he hand-checks you in pass coverage. We're going to have to call the cops."

He stopped apologizing then and said, "Shut up, Jackson."

Everybody laughed, and we resumed playing without further

incident. Just as the girls were about to put us away due to Mc-Dougal becoming overly cautious, the game came to an abrupt end when his mom took it upon herself to have a pizza delivered.

Setting us up with plates and napkins and more drinks, you could tell she really liked us hanging out. And, while McDougal did have that stupid Dollar Store haircut and you could knock him over by breathing on him too hard, he was nowhere as fragile as she thought. Even if you did knock him down, he would always be punching up as he got to his feet.

After the pizza, McDougal dialed up a loop of LCD Soundsystem and we all danced. I'm not really into electronic music or dancing, but LCD had all these cool beats, and songs like "Daft Punk Is Playing at My House" and "Losing My Edge" were really funny. And when the mellowish "I Can Change" found its way into the rotation, I was holding beautiful Lexi in my arms and imagined this was what it was like to defy gravity, to be totally weightless and free. I was further bolstered looking over and seeing my friend McDougal smiling up at Sydney, touching hands, moving to the rhythm of the song. Something weird and wonderful was happening in that stupid garage.

As the day drifted to dusk, Sydney had to get home. She had to babysit her stepsiblings because her parents were going out. We cleaned up the plates and stuff and thanked McDougal's mom for the pizza. She seemed a little disappointed we were leaving, and when McDougal got his bike out to walk us to the corner, she made him promise to wear his helmet. But the helmet wasn't necessary as he sat on his bike ahead of Lexi and me, pushing along with his feet and talking a mile a minute to Sydney. Lexi had wrapped herself around my arm, and it felt good to have her close. McDougal continued on past his corner and turned at Sydney's corner to take her the rest of the way home.

That little bastard. Was there anything he couldn't do?

CHAPTER 6

A FEW DAYS later we got around to looking up some workouts on YouTube. We started slowly doing a circuit routine without any weights in McDougal's garage. Focusing on our lower bodies and cores, we did some basic exercises: squats, lunges, planks, side-arm planks, crunches, burpees, body extensions. Soon, though, we stepped it up, trying new workouts and bringing weights into the mix. McDougal made slow but steady progress, both on the bike and in the workouts, and after a few weeks you could see that his dumb Ninja Turtle workout T-shirt was tightening up. I wouldn't say he had actual muscles or anything, but there was definitely a fuzzy new definition to him. Despite this progress, he had real issues with fatigue where his body would bomb out after a short period of time. He tried to counteract the fatigue with an extra blast of hydrocortisone, but still, what should have been a thirty-minute training session took more than an hour. It was cool hanging out, listening to tunes, and busting chops, and when I got bored waiting on him to recharge, I would do his mom's P90X routine. You had to put up with corny old-guy jokes watching the P90X, but the workouts were beastly and soon I was able to do tons of push-ups, pull-ups, and single-leg squats.

All this training was cutting into the time I spent with Lexi, so she started to come along and work out too. On occasion Skeezy and JuJu, my BMX riding buddies, as well as Denny from Prince's would come by and jump into the rotation. Even though we left Gatorade bottles everywhere and were wreaking havoc on the house—I broke a garage window tossing a football to JuJu, Skeezy skidded into a flower bed and tore up some new buds—McDougal's mom loved us coming over. She worked odd hours at the hospital, so sometimes she wasn't there, but when she was, she would make a point to come out and pick up a bit and invite whoever was there to stay for dinner.

With all this action and people stopping by, there was still some downtime and Lexi, who was forever a C student, started to get some help from McDougal in Algebra and Earth Science. He had taken those classes in eighth-grade and was now doing AP classes in Biology and Geometry. With his help Lexi started getting As right away. Seeing her progress, I started to listen in too, since those were my worst classes, but I only got Bs. My commitment, unlike Lexi's, was lacking since I wasn't huge on studying or homework. If I didn't get it in class—I didn't get it. And, if "on time and complete" was required, that was a problem too. In my mind the Bs averaged out well enough with my good subjects, English and History. I helped Lexi in those classes, mostly just looking over some essays and assignments, and soon enough, for the first time in her life, she was getting As across the board. She was so proud of herself.

Sydney, who was always a topic of conversation, was absent during the week because she had babysitting duties after school, but we continued to do the Saturday thing either at McDougal's house or at The Spot. She seemed to really like hanging with us, but that's as far as it went—hanging out. From the start Lexi had been skeptical about romance between McDougal and Sydney, but when she saw what was happening between them, she thought maybe there was a chance. Sydney, however, had zero interest.

"She laughed when I brought it up," Lexi said.

"C'mon, really? Screw her," I said, angry for McDougal.

"No. She caught herself and apologized for laughing and said all kinds of nice things about James. It's just she doesn't see him in a romantic way."

"Yeah, I get it, but still, screw her."

We debated whether or not to tell him. I was of the opinion that we should, but Lexi argued to give it some time so he could figure it out for himself. We didn't have to wait long for a clue to present itself. She showed up the next Saturday night, her self-imposed exile from guys apparently in the rearview mirror, with this spindly dude from eleventh grade named Gary Clausen. It was immediately awkward and you could tell McDougal was upset. I was pissed too and started right in on this Clausen asshole. First, I asked him how many grades he failed since the name Gary was like from the '60s. He told us it was a family name and he was like a fourth-generation Gary. Next, on McDougal's phone I dialed up "Gary's Got a Boner" by this great band from the '80s, The Replacements. It's a purposely stupid tune, but Clausen said he never heard his name used in a song before and thought it was cool. Then I told him that I read in the band's bio they used that name because all the Garys they ever met were more or less losers.

"So," I said, "four generations of Garys. That's about a hundred years' worth of losers."

"Fuck off Jackson. That's not cool," he said.

Lexi and McDougal turned away smiling, while Sydney bored in on me with those blue eyes. Defending myself, I said, "That's not me saying that. It was an observation by the best band of the '80s, The Replacements. If it was like the '60s, then it would be The Beatles saying it because obviously, they were the best band of the '60s. But like I said, I never met a Gary before and you know, you seem okay to me."

"Yeah, whatever. Syd, let's blow," he said.

Passive aggressively McDougal came to his defense, saying, "Shut up, Jackson. You're the loser." Then, turning to Gary, he said, "Forget Jackson. His middle name is Gary."

But before the jab registered, McDougal was asking him about the bands he liked, and it was no surprise when the asshole named the Red Hot Chili Peppers as his favorite. With multiple piercings in his ears and eyebrows, he also talked about inking himself up. A Sydney type of guy through and through.

In particular, he went on and on about how he was going to get the Native American-inspired tat that Chili Pepper singer Anthony Kiedis had on his back.

"Are you Native American or something?" McDougal asked.

"No, Danish," he said.

"Are you into Native American culture?"

"No. I just like that tat," he said.

"Yeah, but that's Kiedis's tattoo."

"So . . . I like it and when I'm eighteen, I'm doing it."

"Yeah, but isn't body art supposed to represent someone's individuality and be unique to that person? And getting the same tat as Anthony Kiedis defeats the purpose, doesn't it?" McDougal asked very reasonably.

"But it's really cool," he said.

Finally, Sydney joined in and said, "That makes you a follower."

Her body language told me the conversation had really soured her on him, and when it was time to go to some party off of Seneca Street, all of the sudden she remembered she had a project due on Monday that McDougal was going to help her with and she couldn't go to the party. Clausen didn't seem to catch on that she was bull-shitting about the project and took off. Though she chose to hang with us instead of him she was she was kind of mad, especially with me.

"That was not cool, Jackson,"

"C'mon, Syd, the dude's into the Chili Peppers."

"Yeah, so, is that a crime? I'd never do that to you,"

Then that little opportunistic bastard McDougal jumped in. "Jackson, even though Clausen likes different things than us, he's Sydney's friend and we owe it to her to be respectful to whoever she brings around, even if they like the Chili Peppers."

I could hardly believe my ears, but I saw his game, that little gleam in his eye, and instead of busting him on it, I played along and apologized. "Syd, sorry I came on so strong. I won't do that again, even if the person is into the Chili Peppers, but I make no promises if it's, like, U2."

"WTF, Jackson?" McDougal said.

"I'm kidding."

"How 'bout Coldplay? What if they're into Coldplay?" Lexi asked.

McDougal turned to Sydney and said, "Sorry, Syd, that's where we draw the line. Open season on anyone into Coldplay. No mercy whatsoever."

We all laughed and then listened to the latest Diiv record, *Is the Is Are*, and played a raucous game of *Cards Against Humanity*.

Things were mostly smoothed over, but I still felt a little attitude from Sydney playing the game. She sort of stared at me stone-faced, even when I had the response of the year to the question "What brought the orgy to a grinding halt?" with *Child Protective Services.* But that would change walking home.

It was a perfect June night in Buffalo: calm, warm, no humidity. As usual McDougal inched along next to Sydney on his BMX, while Lexi and I trailed behind. When they crossed the Avenue at Sydney's street, the smell of chicken wings coming from Outlaws was powerful. Saying goodbye to them, I had a moment of hot-chicken-wing revelry, which was almost immediately interrupted by some violent yelling and screaming coming from the direction of the bar. We ran across the street and there in front of Outlaws, Sydney was screaming at, of all people, my old man. It was a surreal moment, and it took a second or two for it to really register as little McDougal stood between them with his arms extended, not really pushing on either of them, but still keeping them separate.

"What makes you think you can talk that shit to me?" she screamed.

"When you dress like a whore, people talk to you like a whore."

The old man slapped McDougal's hand away, which caused him to lose his balance and hit the pavement. After that some guy staggered out of the bar and took my old man down on top of McDougal. The guy was really drunk and the old man easily turned him over and started pounding him.

As I came up on them, Sydney was hurling invectives and some useless punches. McDougal was trapped beneath both men yelling, "Dad! Dad! Dad!" I came in low with my shoulder and blew the whole thing up, freeing McDougal and, I guess, his father.

I was up in a flash while the old man slowly lumbered to his feet, yelling, "I'll fucking kill you, Jackson!"

He came at me, but was a flimsy bag of drunken bones, and I locked him up easily, pinning his arms behind his back. The only thing he could really do was curse me out.

By then people had started to file out of the bar. Some lady with a bar rag applied pressure to a cut above McDougal's father's eye and wiped away the trickle of blood from his nose. Besides being pretty drunk, he was mostly fine. McDougal was fine too.

Some big dude from the bar stomped over to where I was holding my old man, who had mostly stopped struggling but was still motherfucking me up and down. My old man was overdressed for the weather in a flannel shirt, and this guy put his hand on his shoulder and from behind a big whiskey-soaked beard said, "It's over, Mickey. Time for you to walk." Then he looked at me and said, "Let him go, son."

I did what the guy asked, and of course, as soon as I released him, the old man spun around and landed a backhand squarely on my jaw and said, "You're dead, Jackson."

But the big guy with the beard and the whiskey voice grabbed a handful of flannel and yanked him away and started to walk him to the corner.

Watching him recede into the dusky twilight as he continued to rant at me, I stood there methodically rubbing my jaw. I wasn't physically hurt, but standing there I had the realization that the misery that was my old man was now extending to my friends. There wasn't any part of my life free from his bullshit and it incredibly demoralizing.

However, when the big guy from the bar got him to the corner, he gave the old man a *get the fuck outta here* shove down the Avenue. That was a very satisfying visual and buoyed my spirit, and I wished I could give him one of those once-and-for-all shoves right out of my life.

After finding McDougal's father's wire-rimmed glasses at the curb, Lexi came and took my hand. Her beautiful, sympathetic eyes brought light to that dark moment, and I was filled with a warm, yet broken kind of happiness and felt very lucky to be with her. Despite being kind of an asshole earlier in the night, Sydney too looked at me with kind eyes. Even though I could barely meet her eyes as I tried unsuccessfully to find words of apology I felt grateful to count her as a friend.

The big guy with the beard and whiskey voice came back toward us and gave me a couple of taps of approval on the shoulder. Then he went over to McDougal's father and said, "Are you all right, Jimmy?"

Besides being drunk, he seemed okay. With his glasses in place he had this professorial air, but otherwise McDougal's old man was an older, more gangly version of McDougal, with mirthful lines creeping out from his eyes, a sunken chest, long fingers, and slip-on shoes. It was all topped with the same bad haircut, purchased in aisle three of the Dollar Store.

After being introduced to all of us and commenting to me that my old man was "one bad dude," he stammered on exuberantly about how Sydney looked like a young Martha Washington. Yes, the first, first lady, but not the old frumpy Martha Washington we've come to know.

"Forensic anthropologists," he explained in a happy drunken voice, "using computer regression software have been able to erase all the wrinkles, chins, and white hair to reveal a beautiful younger version of Martha Washington who had a strong jaw, bright eyes, and chestnut-colored hair, just like you. Here, take a look . . ." He fumbled through his pockets looking for his phone and said, "Must be in the bar. James, let's see your phone."

But McDougal was talking on his phone, saying, "Yeah, he's okay, but maybe you should come to make sure . . . Okay . . . Yes . . . Bye."

He looked up after ending the call, and his dad said, "Lemme see your phone, James."

McDougal handed over his phone, and as his dad clumsily tried to punch up the hot young Martha Washington who looked like Sydney, I found the words to apologize to her.

"I'm really sorry, Syd. My old man is such an asshole."

"That guy in the flannel was your father, huh?"

"Unfortunately, yes."

"Then I'm sorry," she said, and she came over and leaned into me for a mini sort of hug, which I really appreciated. Pulling away and nodding toward McDougal's father, who was still searching for the Martha Washington image, she said, "Seems like we all hit the father jackpot. James's dad here, your old man, Lexi's whose is always MIA, and my stepdad who can't hold a job or even watch his own kids while my mom works."

The point was accentuated by the excitement of McDougal's drunken old man when he finally found the Martha Washington image. "Look . . . Look . . ." he said, first showing it to Sydney and then to the rest of us, even the big guy with the long beard and whiskey voice from the bar, who was heading back inside. And though she did look like Syd, except for the hair—Syd's was redder than the first lady's—it was kind of sad seeing McDougal's old man with his busted-up face focused on something so frivolous.

When McDougal's mom pulled up in her Ford Escape, she was all business. She looked McDougal over quickly, then asked the girls and me if we were all right before moving on to his old man.

Even though his actions were totally honorable, McDougal's old man was like a schoolboy explaining to his mom why he was in trouble again as his ex-wife checked him out. "I looked out the window and saw James struggling with Mickey Wolf. What was I supposed to do? I had to do something."

"It's all right, Jimmy," she said calmly. "James explained every-thing." She finished looking him over and said, "Except for the cut on your eye, you seem fine. Everybody in the car."

We put the BMX bike in the cargo space of the little SUV and piled into the back seat while McDougal's old man sat in the front. First, we dropped Syd off just up the street, and then Lexi. After that Mrs. McDougal informed me that I would be spending the night at their house. Feeling kind of responsible for all the bullshit that went down, I tried to object, but she was not having it. "It's set-tled, Jackson. You're staying at our house. And tomorrow, I'm going to have a conversation with that father of yours."

McDougal's old man was now snoozing in the front seat. Still all business, she pulled up in front of their house and said, "I'm going to take him home, clean him up, and put him to bed. Jackson, you can sleep in the guest room, or you can set up the air mattress in James's room if you want."

McDougal tried to jump in, "Mom, we can help you with . . ."

But with a stern look, she cut him off and ordered us from the car. "Go."

We decided that I would stay in McDougal's room, and while filling up the air mattress, he joked, "You're not going to try and do gay shit to me in the middle of the night, are you?"

"Probably not. I need a man with more than a baby carrot between his legs."

"Your mom didn't think . . ." And then he stopped and, looking away, said, "Sorry."

"Dude, it's cool. That was my shit and it's the past. And my mom, even though she's not around, probably needs more than a baby carrot too."

Smiling, he said, "Screw you, Jackson."

"No, screw you, James."

It was still early, so we decided to listen to some tunes in the garage. McDougal explained when shit like this happens, his mom is usually gone for hours trying to bring some semblance of order to his old man's apartment, which always was a disaster.

Besides the tunes, McDougal had another idea. "Wanna catch a buzz?"

"Umm . . . a buzz?" I said, hesitating.

"Nothing crazy, just a shot and a beer buzz," he said confidently.

I followed him into the neat stainless-steel kitchen, and he retrieved two red sixteen-ounce Solo cups from a cupboard that was built into the wall, grabbed a couple of Labatt Blues from the fridge, and headed to a corner of the dining room where there was a little table with wheels and about twenty bottles of booze: gin, vodka, whiskey, schnapps, the works.

"So it won't be so obvious, we should hit from different bottles. Jim Beam or Jack Daniels?" he asked.

"I'll do the Beam."

The brown whiskey smelled like high-octane cough medicine. I was about to down mine when McDougal put his hand on my arm and said, "Wait . . . It's going to burn and taste really shitty. Just kind of gulp it."

"Oh really, this fucking paint remover is going to taste bad?"

"You're such an asshole Jackson," he said, laughing.

It was even worse than I imagined, but we got them down, did another, poured our beers into the cups, and went out to the garage and sat down in the Adirondack chairs . . . feeling all warm and fine.

McDougal was maybe feeling a little bit more than fine. After messing with his phone a bit, he handed it to me and, slurring, said, "Punch up 'The Sunset Tree' by The Mountain Goats."

I didn't know this record and only half listened to the lonely opening tracks as the night's events tumbled through my mind again. I snapped to attention when the third song, "This Year," started to kick with its jaunty fast-car percussion. It was a sto-ry-song about a kid escaping a broken house to meet a girl named Cathy after boosting his stepdad's car. Both are troubled and are going to make it through *this year*, even if it kills them. I was so able to plug Lexi and I into the narrative, not only the holding-hands, locking-eyes part, but the part where it ends badly at the hands of a stepfather.

I looked over at McDougal, feeling a little set up, but he was snoozing with his barely sipped beer about to fall from his hand. There wasn't much time to think about McDougal—next up was an urgent and haunting cello-based screed that had the tone of a haranguing lecture, followed by a roller-coaster ride of songs with a violent father and a family breaking apart. It all came to a head in the song "Hast Thou Considered the Tetrapod" where the narrator, in the face of the violent sleeping father, boldly affirms, *I'm young and I'm good.* Before my eyes flashed everything happening in my life: Lexi, McDougal, Syd, working out, music, solid grades in school. It was all good. But, of course, the father in the song rises and his misery reigns supreme. And as I sat there next to a snoozing McDougal, all the good things that were coming to me were suddenly canceled out by my old man's never-ending bullshit. I started to cry in a deep, inconsolable way, and was overwhelmed with the crushing sadness that was my life.

CHAPTER 7

B Y THE TIME it was fully dark, I was all cried out and sat sipping the beer remaining in McDougal's cup while he snoozed peacefully in the Adirondack chair. I could hear the faint din of salsa music a street or two over, but otherwise the night remained calm and beautiful. After initially being so crushed by "The Sunset Tree," I cautiously dialed it up for a second listen. I'd been caught off guard the first time, feeling like a mirror had been shoved in front of my face, forcing me to see the ugly sadness of my life. The second spin was different. It generated a grudging acceptance that this was who I was, these were my wounds, and it was up to me to heal myself. And though I could see this battered version of myself in the music, I had no idea what to do with this information besides maybe raging against the old man. Rage would've felt good, but ultimately just seemed stupid and wrong. There had to be some other way to resolve all of this without lowering myself to the old man's level.

When the album was done I solemnly stacked the Adirondack chairs, threw out the paper plates and cups, and closed the garage door. I guided a dazed and confused McDougal to our room, and again he muttered stuff about how I better not do any gay shit to him while he was sleeping. Just before collapsing into bed, he seemed to wake up a bit and gave me a hug, which concluded with three *it'll be all right* pats on the back. He then pushed off his little shorts, fell into bed, and was out cold. I stood there looking at him for a few long moments and decided that the hug wasn't weird. It was nice, in fact, and I appreciated it.

I took off my Vans and lay down on top of the comforter covering the air mattress, and even though I was buzzed and mentally exhausted, sleep would mostly evade me as I thought about the shitstorm that was sure to come at home. Tossing and turning, I tried to come up with a way to bridge the divide between me and the old man without having to resort to violence. It was a hard sell since everything with him was this rigid test of manhood that required you to hate the government, hate the man keeping you down, hate the people stealing your opportunity. It was hate morning, noon, and night, and any disagreement that couldn't be settled with this hate or sneering resentment was settled with an elbow to the gut or a backhand to the head. There were no soft edges to reason with, except maybe through my grandmother, but she was all broken down and busted. Still, if that's all I had, I would have to try and find a way to make it work. I saw no other options. The more I thought about it, the more I knew I was kidding myself. Of course there was going to be violence, but at this point I could hold my own against him, and hopefully I could keep it to a minimum.

Since it was a Sunday, the day we always went to visit my grandmother at the Erie County Home, I would have a chance to put my shaky plan into action straight away. I slipped on my shoes and quietly stepped out into the dewy quiet morning. Walking down the all-but-lifeless Avenue, I heard my phone buzz. I flipped it open and there was a text from McDougal which read, *you are young and you are good . . .* I sat down on the curb looking at the text, and the ugly images of the past night raced through my head. I had an urge to cry again but fought it off. I cried last night—now was the time to act. I got to my feet and was in full agreement with McDougal and The Mountain Goats: I was young and I was good.

All disheveled in the same flannel as the previous night, the old man was waiting on our beat-up couch when I got home. "Where the fuck were you?"

Strangely, not only was I not intimidated, I think I wanted this showdown, and with a little acid in my voice, I said, "You know where I was . . . McDougal's."

"That little retard's house?"

"He's ten times smarter than both of us, and you can't call people retards anymore."

"Who the fuck are you to tell me what I can say?"

"No one, but you sound stupid when you say shit like that."

He sprang up from the couch and got close to my face, still stinking from the previous night. "All I've done for you, you call me stupid in my house?"

Standing my ground, I said incredulously, "You always bring that up . . . All you've done for me? Yeah, if dumping me on Grandma and beating the shit out of me counts as doing something, you've done a lot. And I didn't say you were stupid—I said you *sounded* stupid."

That was it. He unloaded a right cross, which I knocked down easily. That was followed by a flimsy left that brushed the side of my neck while I backed away. Screaming he was going to kill my "ungrateful black ass," he came at me with his arms extended, going for the choke hold, but I grabbed his hands and after a brief struggle I had him wrapped up so he couldn't move. He fought to break my hold as I turned him slightly, plunged my hip into his midsection and took him hard to the living room floor, knocking over a TV table. Then I locked up his legs with mine, leaving him zero wiggle room. Everything but his mouth, which spewed threats and curses at me, was immobilized. I was completely in charge and felt if I squeezed hard enough, I could crush his organs and bones and drain the life from his stinking body. In spite of this feeling of power, I kept it together because I didn't really want to hurt the fucker—I just wanted his shit to stop once and for all.

After some time, he accepted the futility of continuing to struggle. He continued to spew hateful invectives for several more minutes while I remained in complete control. But with the fight gone from his body, he finally said, "Let me go."

"I'll let you go, but there's a couple of things we gotta get straight," I said, still gripping him firmly. "First, you gotta leave my friends alone. Second, you gotta keep your hands off me. I'll stay out of your way, but no more hitting me. No elbows, backhands, fists. Nothing. Okay?"

He started to struggle again, and when he still wasn't able to break my hold, he finally said, "Okay . . . Okay, let fucking go of me."

"All right, but just so we're straight, if you take a swing at me after I let you go, I'm swinging back."

"Yeah, whatever. Lemme fucking go."

After untangling us, I gave him a little push and bounced to my feet, with my hands at my sides but ready.

Lumbering to his feet, he looked old and beaten, his thinning hair a wild mess, his saggy unshaven cheeks drooping as though they wanted to leave his face. The one sign of life was the fire in his watery, bloodshot eyes. Looking at me intently for a moment or two, he then pointed at the TV table that got knocked over and said, "Pick that shit up," and turned to leave. But before I could address the table and the assorted beer cans and cigarette butts strewn all over the floor, he turned back around and said, "I didn't know they were your friends."

Trying to read him, after a moment I said, "McDougal is, but not her so much," inadvertently throwing Sydney under the bus.

"Doesn't surprise me, she's been walking by the bar dressed like a little slut for years. Does she ever smile?"

"What? Yeah, she smiles. She's okay—it's just McDougal likes her and she doesn't like him back, and it pisses me off a little."

"That little fuck . . . Her? Even if he is a wiz, he ain't got a chance in hell with an uppity bitch like that."

"Yeah, probably not."

"You know I know that McDougal kid? Comes into the bar with his crazy nerd father."

I was going to stick up for Sydney and McDougal's old man but decided to let it pass. This little conversation was civility and anything I said in their defense might have sparked more shit. So all I said was, "Yeah, I know." Then I asked, "We going to see Grandma today?"

He paused for a moment, the fire receding from his eyes. "Noon."

Before anything could upset this temporary peace, I got out of there. I went to my room, lay down, and sent McDougal a text. *Thanks for the text and the Mountain Goats. Hit me right between the eyes and I loved it.*

I pressed send, closed my eyes, and got a few hours of sleep.

Except for having to suffer through the sensory assault of Journey's "Don't Stop Believin'" for the billionth time on the classic rock station, the thirty-minute ride to the Erie County Home was uneventful. All cleaned up, the old man seemed a bit dazed behind the wheel, like he was still coming to terms with what happened last night and this morning. Whether there was going to be a shift in how we dealt with each other in the coming days was yet to be determined, but for now I had to make the most of this visit with my grandmother.

During the week, a little bit of my future came into focus when my English teacher, Mr. Cummings, informed me that I had placed third in a national writing contest sponsored by Brown University for a short story I had written at the beginning of the year called "When the Walls Came Down." Mr. Cummings had been telling me even though I was just a freshman, I should be making plans for college and researching scholarship opportunities. I thought he was just blowing smoke, but the award came with a five-hundred-dollar prize to be used toward future educational expenses, and it got me thinking maybe college was a possibility.

McDougal had talked about college almost as a given for the both of us since we started hanging out. It wasn't high-minded talk about us going away to a good software-engineering school or some steeped-in-tradition Ivy League liberal arts institution—it was about girls. He was always doing Google searches on "best colleges to get laid at" or "colleges with the easiest girls," and without fail some degenerate named Damn Boner or DJ Whang would have a list of ten schools, mostly in Texas, where the only thing more plentiful than opioid addiction and rural despair was college girls desperately needing to get laid. For all his ability to see five moves ahead, McDougal's kryptonite was girls and he was totally suckered by these lists.

"You know this Damn Boner guy who came up with this list doesn't exist, don't you?" I said to him.

"Why not? I can hear myself calling out to some dude: Yo Damn or Damneee. Why wouldn't he exist?"

"Okay, fair enough. But there's no way Damneee is traveling around conducting research and compiling data on which campuses have the sluttiest girls."

"I don't know, seems plausible to me that conservative Christian values and the heavy emphasis on abstinence education programs in Texas might translate into a giant mess of ladies down with getting down. Did you know Texas was the last state to decriminalize sodomy?"

"You're a scary little man."

"Scary? Don't you mean noble and selfless? These poor girls are sexually deprived, and out of the goodness of my heart I'm willing to let them defile me. My body will be the life sustaining nutrition they are so deprived of," he said, laughing.

"That body? You're like a half a bag of Skittles on your best day."

"As long as I get eaten, I'll be whatever anyone wants."

"Like I said . . . scary."

Though we talked about college mostly by way of McDougal's perviness, with him there was never a question about me being worthy of higher education—it was a given. When I was young, I read a lot with my mom and Mr. Nate, but after she left and I moved in with my grandmother, she didn't make such a big deal about school or reading and never really got after me when my grades were bad. Of course, the old man was one of those anti-intellectual Fox meatheads who thought liberal college professors were pushing a secret agenda that would lead to Obama's socialist takeover. So, I never really thought about college as a possibility for me until McDougal and this award.

The story itself only came about because I was missing a whole bunch of work in Mr. Cummings's class, and he said he would let it slide if I wrote him a short story . . . a good short story. Not knowing what to do or how to write a short story, I had this idea to write a spoof of the *Book of Revelations*, which was relevant to me at the time because I had been picking through some of those crazy "End Times" novels. I also had recently seen the movie *Goodfellas* and really liked Joe Pesci and thought who better to wreak havoc on humanity than Joe Pesci. So I made him an angel of the apocalypse who administered justice with a baseball bat. Of course, for continual crimes against humanity, the antichrist had to be a classic rock artist. I toyed with Billy Joel and Steven Tyler but settled on Don Henley, for the enduring psychic pain of "Hotel California." It was a beautiful bloody mess, but with a point.

I liked stories and songs that were multidimensional. The best ones would be both funny and sad with characters that were maybe boastful, yet vulnerable too. In my mind, a good story had to be infused with light and dark, and I tried to make my *Book of Revelations* spoof bloody but uplifting, while also making a point. Beyond the magic of Joe Pesci's bat, the 144,000 people to be saved were not the faithful or devout sheep that were always looking to the sky for deliverance. No, the ones who would make it looked out for others and found faith and devotion in arts and sciences. They were people who questioned the existence of God. They dug into the forensics of life and demanded peer-reviewed verifiable facts to back shit up, even for the existence of God. And God, who didn't become divine by looking up to the sky in search of deliverance or by kneeling in some pew to demonstrate piety and loyalty, would accept nothing less. God liked people who put their shoulder to life and made their own destiny. For the rest, there was Joe Pesci.

I brought the award letter and story with me to the Home to show my grandmother and to lay the groundwork for college. I thought if I could use my grandmother's better nature, that might blunt the old man's anger and cynicism. It might have been better to wait, but given what had happened this morning, I felt the need to keep pressing, to strike while the irons were still glowing hot.

It was another nice, warm day and we wheeled my grand-mother out into a little courtyard that needed some sprucing up. The old man and I settled into some depressing plastic chairs while my grandmother sat in her wheelchair, wrapped in a brownish-orange afghan. Her speech was severely limited, and looking so beat, she barely responded to our small-talk inquiries about how she was and what she had been doing. Week after week we asked the same things, and it was the dumbest line of questioning ever, since she could do next to nothing. But thankfully, as I had hoped, she lit up and made happy cooing sounds when I shared my news about the story and the prize money.

As expected, the old man wasn't quite as impressed. "Five hundred dollars for a piece of shit like that? No wonder this country is going to hell."

"Yeah, you know 'cause you're up on all the greats: Chekhov, Steinbeck, Larry the Cable Guy," I shot back.

"Don't be talking shit about Larry. And I don't know them, but I do know when something sounds like a piece of shit."

Shaking my head dismissively, I turned to my grandmother and said, "Mr. Cummings, my English teacher, said I should be looking into colleges and researching . . ."

"Who the fuck are you shaking your head at?" the old man said, standing up aggressively. "You elitist little prick."

"Whaddya talking about?"

"Shaking your head like you're better than me."

Standing up and raising my voice, I said, "I shook my head because, as usual, rather than taking pride or being happy for something I accomplished, you piss all over it."

"That's an accomplishment? A stupid Joe Pesci story?"

"The people at Brown University thought it was pretty good."

"Fucking East Coast eggheads. Whadda they . . .?"

Then, out of the blue, with unmistakable fury, my grandmother yelled, "MICKEY!"

He stopped mid-sentence and his anger turned to red-faced humiliation as my grandmother trembled beneath her blanket, her eyes burning.

A second later he said, "Fuck this," and then he turned and left.

With the old man's exit, my grandmother calmed down quickly. I apologized for upsetting her and a tired, kind smile came to her lips while she shook her head, indicating there was no need to apologize.

I took her hand and softly started to tell her more about school and my plans for the future. By the time I got around to talking about Lexi, McDougal, and Sydney, she had dozed off. I wheeled her back to the foyer, which was filled with warm sunlight pouring through the foggy glass ceiling. She woke up long enough to signal that she was thirsty, and I was able to get her a can of ginger ale from the enthusiastic receptionist at the front desk. She took a few sips through a straw and then dozed off again.

Sitting there next to my snoring grandmother, I had to figure out how to get home. I thought about calling McDougal or Lexi, thinking one of their moms could pick me up, but that would be a huge hassle and I didn't want to impose. Then I went up to the front desk and asked the receptionist if there was a bus that could get me close to South Buffalo. I made up some bullshit about my old man having to attend to an emergency, which I could see she wasn't buying.

Looking at the computer screen, she punched some keys, clicked her wireless mouse, checked the screen for a moment, and then raising her eyes to mine, said, "No, the last metro left at noon today." She looked me over for a moment as if assessing me and then said, "I'm going to South Buffalo, but I'm here till 8 p.m. Let me see if Lenny is here—he'd be leaving at three."

Lenny was one of the maintenance guys, and he was there and he did give me a ride home. Standing there, I was struck by how the receptionist managed that desk, taking calls, handing out keys, having people sign in and out of a logbook, all while solving my problem.

Her name was Jessica Lee and she was doing a masters in social work with a concentration in gerontology at the University of Buffalo. Next semester she was doing an internship at the Erie County Home, and she got this volunteering gig so she could hit the ground running. It was rather amazing—she wasn't being paid, yet she seemed like she was doing the work of five people.

"What's gerontology?" I asked, feeling kind of stupid.

"Gerontology is the study of aging. A gerontological social worker is someone who connects and coordinate resources for the elderly population," she said while putting some charts in a little cart on wheels.

"That's a real job . . . Gerenlogical social worker?"

"Geron*to*logical social worker . . . Of course it's a real job. Did you ever hear of baby boomers? Seventy-six million post-World War II people in the later stages of life who need help with health care, housing, transportation and a million other things."

"Why this? You're so young and . . ." I was going to say pretty, but that wasn't cool. Still, she was attractive, and one of the things that made her attractive was the way she was so in command behind that desk.

"That's your grandmother, Ms. Wolf?" she said, looking in the direction of my snoozing grandma.

"Yes."

"I had a grandmother too, and for many complicated reasons, her last years were pretty dark and lonely. It broke my heart, but rather than be consumed by the mistakes my family made, I decided to do what I could to help people not make those same mistakes. And here I am," she said with confidence.

I looked at her for a second and a thousand more questions came into my head, but she was busy and I didn't want to be a pain, so I thanked her for the help and grabbed a *Time* magazine with Bernie Sanders on the cover and sat back down next to my sleepy grandma.

I was really taken with this Jessica Lee, and between magazine articles, I covertly watched her run that desk with such competence.

She seemed to know and have an answer for everything and when she didn't, she punched something up on her computer or made a call. I was really impressed, not so much at the work she was doing as how she was doing it.

What also struck me was the way she was making some tragic thing from her personal life right with education. In that moment, with my first real educational triumph on sheets of paper rolled up in my hand, that was powerful. I thought education was about a job and skills, but this Jessica Lee showed me there was more to it than just a job. That, in fact, education provided boundless possibilities.

CHAPTER 8

THE OLD MAN was on the porch with a Keystone Light and a cooler when Lenny from the Erie County Home dropped me off. I walked by him without saying a word or making eye contact and went up to my room and lay down on my hastily made bed. I forgot to bring my phone to the Home, and when I looked at it there were a couple of "WHAT HAPPENED WITH YOUR OLD MAN" texts screaming at me from Lexi and McDougal. I thought back over the day and responded: *Little dustup this morning, but think we came to an understanding . . . All good for now.*

Waiting for them to hit me back, I reached under my bed for my library copy of *The Sound and the Fury* by William Faulkner and read a few paragraphs. Normally the library only lets you renew twice, but I've had that book the entire school year. There really wasn't any demand for it, and Ms. Berry, one of the Dudley librarians, and I had been going through it the whole year. Actually, it was more like I would read some and then Ms. Berry explained what I read. I needed a half year of explanations to understand why this piece of shit was a classic. I guess the stream-of-consciousness style pushed literary boundaries the same way Joy Division and Radiohead pushed the boundaries of pop music back in the day. It was still hard to understand, but I was getting it or at least getting something. Same was true of Joy Division and Radiohead—though

I didn't much like them, I knew there was something of value there.

Both Lexi and McDougal wanted to know if it got physical with the old man. As I was explaining about the morning throwdown and the argument that led him to leave me at the Home, McDougal's mom pulled up in front of my house. Watching her get out of the Escape in her blue hospital scrubs from my bedroom window, I was kind of panicked and didn't know what to do. She'd said she was going to stop by and talk with the old man, but I thought that was just something she said in the heat of the moment. All but paralyzed, I sent texts to Lexi and McDougal explaining the situation and asked what I should do. They had opposite opinions. Lexi said engage and McDougal said sit back, his mom knew how to deal with these situations. I took McDougal's advice, but was nervous and paced back and forth for what seemed like an hour. In reality it was like fifteen or twenty minutes, and right after I heard the *thud* of her car door slamming shut and watched her pull away, the old man called to me, "Jackson."

Sluggishly, I made my way down our puke-green, tearing-at-the-edges carpeted stairs, mentally preparing for another battle, but when I got there, the old man had this blank look on his face.

"Yeah?" I said.

"McDougal's mom was here. She said lots of good things about you."

"Like what?"

"Doesn't matter. Look . . . Just stay outta my way and we'll be fine." He then paused like he was going to say something else, but couldn't find the words and finally just said, "Got it?"

"Got it," I said, but I really didn't get it. The tone and the expression on his face was a departure from his usual anger or the occasional humility my grandmother could provoke. I still could sense his explosive pride bubbling just beneath the surface, but for now it was tempered by the events of the last twenty-four hours and the visit of McDougal's mom. Whatever it was, I was very happy for the possibility of peace.

Although there was some tension over petty stuff, like when I forgot to take the trash to the curb on garbage day or when I used all the hot water to shower, the only potential blowup came the night Trump gave his speech at the Republican National Convention. The old man was pretty drunk and from our front porch was yelling, "Vote with your middle finger, America . . . Make America great again . . . Lock her up . . . Lock her up . . . Lock her up . . ." and when I tried to get him to tone it down a bit, he got that look on his face like he was going to come after me. But just as it was about to get rough, the cops showed up and he got himself right and was actually kind of funny with them. There were two officers in separate cars, and he tried to get them to high-five and join him in a "TRUMP . . . TRUMP . . . TRUMP" chant.

The bigger of the two officers seemed to know him and said, "Mickey, we appreciate your enthusiasm, but you're going to have to tone it down. You're pissing off your neighbors."

"Okay . . . okay," he said, and then while pumping his fist, in a low voice he continued to chant, "Trump . . . Trump . . . Trump."

Otherwise, all was good and the summer started with a bang. The last day of school we pulled another gangster heist at Rite Aid, only this time we enlisted Lexi and Sydney because there was extra staff in the store. Lexi persuaded the cashier, who we saw around at school but didn't know, to go back to cosmetics to help her find plum lipstick, and Syd lured the assistant manager to help her search for some faux hair product while McDougal dragged the manager to look for the same imaginary vitamins as the last time. And like the last time, the execution was seamless. McDougal flicked the lights and jammed the security cameras, and I went in and grabbed two sixes of Labatt Blue tallboys, two bags of Rold Gold honey-mustard pretzels, a tin of Altoids, a Bic lighter, and a few plastic bags. In the little entrance/exit vestibule at the front of the store, I put the stuff in the bags and at a quick but cool pace made my way back to The Spot.

It was a beautiful day, and while waiting on them I got the lighter out and started a fire in the rusted-out drum with all the papers and folders in my book bag from my just-cleared-out locker. I shook my head and wondered why I kept this shit all year long. In the distance I could see McDougal between Lexi and Syd with big smiles on their faces. He made broad gestures with his oversized hands and was probably explaining how he jammed the cameras while scamming the Rite Aid manager. Seeing them through the fence like that, seemingly so happy, I had the urge to climb up and yell, "Hurry, motherfuckers," but instead just took them in for a moment and was filled with so much joy I was on the verge of tears. I couldn't really explain this rush of emotion—maybe it was the summery last day of school, the peace that seemed to be holding at home, or my friends who were coming to mean so much to me. Even Syd, who I had bonded with after the fight in front of Outlaws. Though overwhelmed, I managed to keep it together as I held open the fence for them. Once they were through I kissed Lexi and hugged Syd, and then picked McDougal up at the waist and raised him in the air and yelled, "THE MAN!"

He was so funny while I had him up there, extending his arms into a V like a rock star in front of eighty thousand crazed fans. When I set him down, we all grabbed beers, hit the tabs, and raised them up. Lexi led us in a toast: "One, two, three summer." Laughing in unison, we knocked our beers together and it was on—summer.

We all took our first wincing sips, and Syd said, "This is horrible," and then took another giant gulp, making us all laugh.

The girls proceeded to add to the fire with the contents of their book bags while McDougal dialed up some old-school "Interstate Managers" by Fountains of Wayne on the Bluetooth, which was a great sprinkle-covered ice-cream-cone, top-of-the-pops summertime selection.

At the bottom of her book bag, Lexi found the pack of Smokin' Joes menthols she'd nipped from her mom back when we pulled the first Rite Aid heist months earlier.

"I meant to give them back to her but kept forgetting."

"Are they still good?" Syd asked.

I took the pack and smelled them. I'm not sure what exactly I thought I was going to glean from putting them up to my nose. Then I said, "I see the old man pull dirty butts from the ashtray all the time. These are fine."

Everyone took one and I lit them. And like we laughed in unison after toasting the summer, we all coughed at the same time after hitting the smokes.

"These are awful," McDougal said.

"Yeah, but look, I'm Audrey Hepburn from *Breakfast at Tiffany's*," Syd said, lowering the prodigious shades sitting on her head and smiling broadly as she casually raised the cigarette to her lips.

"Audrey Hepburn?" I asked.

First looking at Lexi and then at me, Syd pulled up her shades and said, "You don't know Audrey Hepburn?"

"I know who she is. It's just kind of an ancient reference, isn't it?"

"I watched that DVD a million times with my mom," Lexi said. "Audrey Hepburn is so feisty and elegant in that movie."

McDougal set his oversized beer on the ground and took Sydney's hand. Channeling his inner George Peppard, he said, "No one is more exciting and elegant than you," and then he kissed her hand.

"Oh come on, McDougal, you had like two sips of beer."

Both girls responded at the same time, "Shut up, Jackson," and then looking sweetly back at McDougal, Syd said, "Continue, James."

"The sunshine that falls from the heavens is only rivaled by the brilliance of your smile. The soft summer breezes exist only to blow gently through your hair. The wildflowers strong and free in the field count you as their own. All who have sight marvel at the blue electricity of your eyes. All who can hear are charmed and made wiser by your words . . ."

Sydney was enchanted by these lines, to say the least, and so was Lexi and quite frankly, so was I. Then Syd's phone started to blow up. She ignored it at first, but when it continued to buzz she reluctantly looked at it and said, "Oh fucking Christ, it's my stepfather. He's asking where I am and when I'm coming home. Says my brother and sister are starving and need lunch." And sitting down on a milk crate, clearly frustrated, she continued, "That lazy piece of shit, can't even slap some peanut butter and jelly between two slices of bread." She then lowered her head between her hands and shrieked, "EEEEUUCCK . . ."

McDougal pulled up a crate and sat down next to her and with a certain raw charisma said, "Let me see your phone." She handed it over and with a couple of bold taps he powered it down and dropped it into her book bag, which was in front of her. "You do a lot for your family. You've earned a few hours with your friends on the last day of school."

"Hackensack," a slow, moody number with plush harmonies about some sad-sack kid vowing to wait for an old high-school flame, floated from the Bluetooth and fit the moment perfectly in an ironic kind of way.

Lexi went over and wrapped her aviators around McDougal's ears, roughed up his hair, and then lit another smoke and handed it to him. She sat back down next to me and said, "Syd is Audrey Hepburn from *Breakfast at Tiffany's*, and James is Brad Pitt's character in *Fight Club*."

"Tyler Durden," I said.

"Yeah, that's McDougal today: Tyler Durden."

And McDougal didn't miss a beat. Standing up, gesturing with his cigarette, his black T-shirt clinging to his taut little muscled chest, he said, "The first rule of The Spot is: you don't talk about The Spot. The second rule of The Spot is: you DO NOT talk about The Spot. The third rule of The Spot is: don't yell or play the music too loud and you don't make the fire too big . . . All this jeopardizes The Spot. Be cool to The Spot and The Spot will be cool to you."

McDougal and I traded lines from the movie about *your life draining away a minute at a time* and *the things you own, eventually owning you* and *losing everything makes you free to do anything*.

"I liked that movie and Brad Pitt as the tough street philosopher," Lexi said, "but I saw it again not long ago, and I don't know, it felt like a bunch of snowflake white guys complaining about their loss of privilege."

Well into her second beer, Syd said, "Exactly. And how do white guys always solve their problems? They beat the shit out of things. Usually it's us. At least in the movie they beat the shit out of each other."

"Fucking white guys. Explain yourself, McDougal," I said with fake outrage.

"Wow, that got dark fast," he said, smiling. After pausing for a moment, he thoughtfully answered, "I never saw it that way, but Lexi and Syd are right. White guys have had their way all through history, maiming and killing and taking anything they wanted. It's not hard to see how something like *Fight Club* might be a precursor to all this Trump bullshit and white guy loss of privilege."

"Yeah, but *Fight Club* cuts below the surface and tries to hit at some underlying psychological shit, which is not what I saw when the old man dragged me to the Trump rally. That was a mob of white people out for blood," I said.

"So, this means *Fight Club* sucks now?" McDougal asked.

"Nah . . . maybe," Lexi said without much certainty. "One thing for sure is Trump sucks."

"Not according to my old man," I said.

"Yeah, mine too," said Syd.

"Mine too," said Lexi.

"My mom has been for Hillary all along, and my dad . . . he's for vodka," McDougal said, making us all laugh.

Opening her third beer and slurring a bit, Syd looked at me and said, "Hopefully when Hillary wins, all you white dudes will get in line."

"I ain't white, why you looking at me?"

"Your old man is the whitest fucker on the planet and you got some of that."

Just then "Hey Julie," with its head-bopping, finger-snapping percussion, came up on the Bluetooth, and I stood up and started to dance. "Can a white man move like this?"

They all laughed, and McDougal, who still had some papers in his book bag crumpled a few up and threw them at me.

"Oh my god, you are beyond awful. This is proof you're a lame white guy, Jackson," Lexi said. She stood up and in full smile mode took my hands and said, "Follow my feet."

Sydney and McDougal then got up too and Syd said, "James is bad, but not as bad as you Jackson."

Next up was "Halley's Waitress," a slow number, perfect for holding and breathing in Lexi's goodness. After that was a country romp, and again Lexi had me follow her steps as best I could, but I was truly awful and unfocused because all I wanted to do was take Lexi in, which made it hard to execute the task at hand.

Syd and McDougal hung in there too. They were laughing and having a good time as McDougal, like me, tried to learn some steps.

But then "Fire Island," another gorgeous slow song, found its way into the rotation. Looking into each other's eyes, Lexi and I found a gentle hand-touching rhythm. When the chorus came in with lines about being old enough and not needing our parents, I felt really connected to her and suddenly three words were on the tip of my tongue, but before I could say them Syd, who was all tangled in a slow dance with McDougal, leaned over and started to kiss him . . . really kiss him. I nudged Lexi to look, and a big ear to ear smile rose on her face. A second later Syd was leading McDougal to the side of the building, out toward the weedy parking lot where they could make out in private.

Laughing, Lexi and I sat down next to each other. I leaned over and picked up Syd's beer. It was her third one and was almost empty. I was feeling buzzed halfway through my second and said, "I think Syd is feeling pretty good."

"Yeah, when she does something, she does it all the way."

"Will she get shit for this?"

"Probably, but it's good she pushes back. Her stepfather is worthless."

"Booze?"

"Nah, more OTB and coffee with his buddies at Tim Horton's, while her mom works a chair at Supercuts and Syd is with the kids."

McDougal had taken his phone with him to the side of the building where he was making out with Syd. He was too far from the Bluetooth, so we had no tunes. Lexi put her crate in front of mine, and I wrapped my arms around her as she leaned back into my chest. She had gotten her aviators back from McDougal, and looking up at the sky wispy with summer clouds, she said, "What a perfect last day of school."

As I felt her warm curvy body against mine, what I was going to say earlier came back to me. "Before the McDougal and Syd show, I was about to tell you something."

Sitting up and turning her head, she said, "Wait," and then she swung her body around and faced me. "Go ahead."

Her sitting up and facing me sort of changed the mood, and I stumbled for words. "Lexi, I have so much fun with you and you're so beautiful and smart . . . and we're so good together . . . I think

I . . ."

"You think you love me?" she said, cutting me off. She moved the aviators to the top of her head and with a concerned look on her face said, "Is that it? . . . You love me?"

"Jesus Christ, Lexi. A moment ago maybe, but what the fuck?"

Taking my hands, she said, "Jackson, I'm really sorry. I think I love you too. But can we not do this?"

"Whaddya talkin' about?"

"This . . . Us."

"Again, whaddya talkin' about?"

"Can we not say that word?"

"What word?"

"Lemme explain. Remember that kid I went out with before you, Ted Groman?"

"The white dude with the afro who always wears the Big Star tee . . . yeah."

"Well, we were in love too. At least we thought we were. Once the *love* word was out there, we sort of bludgeoned each other with it. Every time I didn't text him back within two minutes, he'd say I took his love for granted, and every time he'd say something sarcastic, I'd get mad and say he was abusing our love. It got to be this stupid toxic thing. So can we just not use that word?"

Laughing, I said, "That's some real Dr. Phil bullshit there."

"Jackson."

"But you love me."

"Jackson," she said, changing the tone of her voice, and then she leaned in and kissed me.

As we separated from the kiss, Lexi's eyes fixated on something behind me. I turned my head and it was McDougal coming at us at a good clip.

"Sydney just threw up," he said, a little winded.

"Is she all right?" Lexi asked.

"McDougal, what did you do to that girl?"

"Ha ha, jackass. She's fine but wants some water. Can you guys get some from Rite Aid?" he said, holding a ten-dollar bill in his hand.

"Sure," I said. "Lexi, why don't you stay and I'll just run and get it?"

It was agreed upon and I sprinted through the field and parking lot to the store. When I returned they were all sitting together on the crates and McDougal was holding white-faced Syd's hand.

I sat down and pulled a water out of the bag and handed it to Syd, saying, "I got some Gatorades too."

"Thank you, Jackson," she said, sounding defeated.

With McDougal still holding her hand, she stood up and took a few wobbly steps. She drank some water, swished it around in her mouth, and then spit it out. She repeated this process a couple of times, then sat down and said, "I feel so stupid."

Both Lexi and McDougal said comforting things while I made a crude joke about McDougal being two sips away from blowing chow too, for which I was roundly rebuffed.

As Syd chilled, sipping more water and some Gatorade, McDougal dialed up a chill summer mix with songs by Chuck Prophet and Josh Rouse. Coming down from our buzzes, we talked and laughed. All was good again.

To be perfectly honest, I thought the chances of McDougal kissing the beautiful Sydney Cheever, was a long shot, like the Bills winning the Super Bowl or the Sabres winning the Stanley Cup, but

I'll be damned if it didn't happen. Okay, it took a few beers, but he patiently played a long game and made it a reality.

Once again, I was thoroughly amazed at the force of nature that was McDougal.

CHAPTER 9

McDOUGAL REMAINED EXTREMELY attentive to Syd throughout the remainder of the afternoon as she sobered up, while Lexi and I cautiously sipped our beers and caught a moderate buzz. We listened to more tunes and were very taken by the rocking new Car Seat Headrest record, *Teens of Denial*. With all our school papers burned, we used the rusted-out drum to play several improvised games of KanJam. Even buzzing, Lexi was clearly the best among us, setting up whoever was her partner with easy slams after near-perfect throws. During this part of the game, with the sun at their backs, both girls cut exquisite figures as thin shards of light fragmented from behind their lean bodies. A couple of times McDougal and I just kind of looked at each other and were amazed these girls were here with us.

Eventually, the power ran down on the Bose speaker and we sobered up the rest of the way, eating the pretzels, drinking the Gatorades, and downing the Altoids. Except for the little blip of Syd vomiting, it had been a great fun day, a perfect day. The kind of day Lou Reed would sing about after drinking sangria in the park. Syd wasn't feeling the good vibes like the rest of us, still a little embarrassed and paranoid about vomiting and before turning down her street, she asked Lexi to check her breath. "I'm going to get enough shit for not coming home. I can't get caught drinking too."

Lexi leaned in, assessing her. "You're Altoid perfect. You should be good." Then she gave Syd a hug.

Talking about what a fun day it was, we all exchanged hugs, even McDougal and me. He got a big laugh from saying, "Jackson, you can't put your hand there."

After separating from them, Lexi and I walked the couple of blocks to her house in relative silence. We talked a bit about how crazy it was that Syd and McDougal got together, but there was something on her mind. "Whatever it is, you can tell me."

She took a deep breath, her eyes growing big for a second, and then after briefly pausing said, "Never mind, not now."

But when we got to her house and were sitting on her front steps, I could tell this thing was still bugging her. "C'mon, Lex, tell me."

"Not now."

"Lexi."

She paused for a second and then said, "Okay, but it's complicated and you might get mad. Promise me you won't get mad."

"I can't promise that."

"Okay . . . right. Then promise me that if you do get mad and feel the need to stomp away or something, you'll take some time to think about what I'm telling you. Like in *To Kill a Mockingbird*, walk around in my skin and think about it."

Smiling, I said, "You're going Atticus Finch on me?"

"Promise."

"Okay, okay . . . I promise."

She paused again and then began, "Remember earlier in the day when we were talking about the *love* word and were interrupted by Sydney's issues?"

"Yeah, of course, I've been thinking about it all day. I'm cool—we don't have to use the word. This thing between us can be all Zen."

She smiled sweetly and said, "Great, but there's more."

"Okay."

She stood up and, looking down at me sitting on the steps, said, "I don't want to be a jerk about this, but besides not using the *love* word, we have to go really, really slow."

"Okay, I understand."

"No, I don't think you do. Stuff happened with Ted and we have to talk about it."

"Like what, he wanted his Big Star vinyl back?" I said, trying to give the conversation a lighter touch.

"Jackson, this is serious."

"Okay . . . okay."

"So, like I said before, we bludgeoned each other with the *love* word in this really toxic way. And although I was angry and disappointed much of the time we were together, I really loved the guy and was crushed when we broke up. I cried and cried and walked around like a zombie for weeks. I can't do that again."

"That doesn't have to happen with us."

"You say that, but it's not just this simple choice of doing one thing instead of another. Like I'll walk home this way instead of that way. It's more complicated."

"I guess I'm not getting what you're saying."

"Okay, I can be more specific. So, you know my house is messed up. My mom is single and always stressed, my dad isn't really around, and my little brother is kind of a pain in the ass. We get by, but it's not this well-oiled machine where quirky things happen and it all works in the end, like on *Modern Family*. Lots of times things are just totally messed up."

"Oh yeah, I know something about that."

"So then Ted enters the scene and I fall for him hard. And soon enough, the love I feel for him washes away all the messed-up stuff in the rest of my life. It's intoxicating and my head spins and I never, ever think of the downside. Then, folding laundry in the basement with my headphones on, I don't see a text for an hour. I answer when I see it, but the damage has been done and all this resentful bullshit comes back at me. We get by it, but not really. Before long I start to find things to resent too and fling my bullshit at him. He counters and before you know it we're fighting all the time and eventually we break up, unleashing this unbearable pain that makes me walk the earth as a stupid crying zombie girl for a month."

"Ahh, now I get it." And then, after thinking about it for a second, I said, "But we're good. We don't have those things."

"Yeah, Ted and I didn't have those things either until we started to throw the *love* word around."

"But we already decided how to deal with it."

"I know, but it's more than just the word. These feelings can be so overwhelming, and we both come from such messed-up houses. I'm just scared."

"That's it, isn't it?" I said, a light going off in my head. "My situation at home is so bad, you're scared I won't be able to handle being in love. I'll be like one of those assholes who never had money, then wins the lottery and squanders it all on booze and hookers."

"Not the most elegant comparison, but yeah," she said, her voice trailing off.

"Sorry . . . and . . . *wow*. Holy shit, Lexi." I got to my feet, astonished at this turn in the conversation.

"Are you mad?"

"No, I'm not mad. I'm just . . . *wow*. What the hell am I sup-posed to do with that?"

"You're supposed to think about it and try to see it from my point of view. I went in so blind last time and got crushed for it. I can't do that again." After a long pause, as I continued to stand there with my head exploding, she leaned in and kissed me and said, "I had the best time today. I'm so happy to be with you." She turned and started up the porch steps, and when she was at the top, she stopped and said, "Think about it and call me."

I turned away from her house in a daze and started walking. The word *wow* kept popping into my head as I tried to make sense of what Lexi had just said. When I regained my bearings, I realized I had overshot my street. But instead of turning around, I just continued on to McDougal's house. Not only could he help me sort this out, but I also had to find out what happened with Syd.

Coming out of my haze walking down McDougal's street, I did start to get a little mad at Lexi. Part of it was stupid, part of it not. The stupid part was I got mad simply because she was with someone else. I knew it was dumb to get mad about something in the past that couldn't change, but it killed me to think of her be-ing in love with that Groman kid. Less stupid was I put myself out there and she shut me down before I could even express myself. I mean, I'm sorry she went through all that shit, but that wasn't my shit—that was Groman's shit. Why was I picking up the tab for that asshole? Screw him, his white-boy afro, and all his Big Star bullshit.

With the garage door up and no SUV, I knew McDougal was home but not his mom. Fueled by my sketchy anger, I banged on the door inside the garage maybe a little too aggressively. A moment later he answered, and his stupid Dollar Store hair was a bigger mess than usual, dark shades covered his eyes, and one of the unlit menthols dangled from his lips. He leaned against the doorframe, folded his arms, and said, "Durden. Tyler Durden."

All of my silly anger instantly dissolved. We high-fived and I continued in *Fight Club* mode. "You are not your size—you are not your grades. You are not your bike, your phone, or even your stupid haircut. You are a *horngry* young man providing a healthy alternative to girls from dysfunctional homes."

He came down the steps into the garage and we jumped to high-five again, and McDougal's hand landed about the middle of my forearm. Laughing as we came out of it, he said, "That's pretty good, but I'm an alternative for *hot* girls from dysfunctional homes."

Pulling a couple of chairs out, I agreed, "Syd is pretty goddamn hot."

"Dude, you have no idea."

Sitting down, I asked, "So, what turned her?"

"Not sure . . . Music, beer, charisma."

"Beer, yes . . . Music, yes . . . Charisma, eeh . . ."

"Whatever. All I know is we're dancing and she starts saying all this shit to me about how nice I am, how I help her in art class, how sweet it is I walk her home, how I would never just pull up to her house and beep for her, like other guys. Shit like that, and I didn't say anything. I just went with the Tyler Durden cool thing. And then she starts kissing me."

I smiled and put up my hand for a fist bump. Smiling too, McDougal bumped my fist, but before he continued, a look of concern grew on his face and he said, "Hey man, I really care about her, so whatever I tell you stays between us."

"Yeah, yeah . . . Between us and all my Facebook, Twitter, and Snapchat friends."

"Jackson, c'mon man . . . I care about her and don't want to be one of those assholes."

A little miffed, I said, "I mean, could this story really be that good?"

"Oh, it's pretty good."

"Lexi?"

He paused, then said, "Not even Lexi, but Syd will probably tell her."

"What if Lexi brings it up to me?"

"That's cool, I suppose," he said, still looking worried.

"What'd you do to her? You're all tweaked out."

"No . . . no. It's good. Just promise."

"Okay, okay, I promise. Everybody wants a goddamn promise from me today."

He gave me a long assessing look and then continued. "So, we're dancing and I got this Tyler Durden thing going and she starts to kiss me. I'm real aggressive because what do I know about kissing? That's when she takes my hand and we go to the side of the building . . ."

"And she pukes?"

"No, that's not when she pukes," he said, looking around like someone might be eavesdropping. "At the side of the building she tells me to relax and follow her. She starts kissing me again, and unlike me and all my flailing-around bullshit, she knows what she's doing, moving her tongue around in my mouth like an artist or something."

"Then she pukes?"

"No, shut up and let me tell the goddamn story," he said all
Tyler Durden-like. He looked around again and continued in a
voice just above a whisper. "So, she's like Picasso, her tongue paint-
ing all this wild shit in my mouth, and it's the greatest fucking thing
ever. Only that's not all. She becomes more intense, insistent even,
in the way she's kissing, and I can tell she's getting worked up." He
stopped, looked around again . . . "Then, while kissing me so insis-
tently, she takes my hands and puts them on her chest."

"No way. The good part of her chest?"

"The great part of her chest."

"Under or over the shirt?"

"Over, but it doesn't matter. I'm like out-of-my-mind excited . . .
and too aggressive."

"Then she pukes?"

"No, shut up about the puking. So she takes my hands and
slows them down, and I find this nice rhythm, and after a little bit
she starts making these sexy little whimpering sounds that have me
going out of my mind."

"She pukes now?"

Frustrated, he raised his voice and said, "No. She puts her hand
on my dick and starts to rub."

"No way," I said slowly, shaking my head.

"Really. She put her hand on my dick and rubbed."

I could see he wasn't bullshitting and said, "Get the fuck out of
here?"

He nodded, a big smile coming to his face. "I shit you not."

"So what happens?"

"Aw man, I'm crazy excited, and you know . . . I lose my shit."

"No fucking way."

"Dude, seriously . . . Oh, and then she pukes."

"That is unbelievable," I said, marveling at the little shit. "You got over on Sydney Cheever."

"Don't say it like that."

"Still."

"Yeah, I guess, but I like her. And you're going to keep your mouth shut, even to Lexi, right?"

"Hell yes. Shit, I've been with lots of girls and never got that kind of action. It'd be too embarrassing to tell anybody you got worked over below the belt the first time you stepped into the batter's box."

Laughing, he said, "Hey, not everyone can be Derek Jeter."

"You're such an asshole," I said, smiling. Then a thought occurred to me. "I changed my mind—I have to tell Lexi. Ya know, to get her to step it up."

"Jackson."

"No, seriously. Here I am doing all this dutiful boyfriend shit, and I maybe get a little second-base action here and there, while Syd takes you along for a stand-up triple. It's bullshit."

Turning a little downcast, he said, "Well, you know she was kind of bombed and freaked about puking and . . ."

"Aw c'mon, Jeter . . . Durden. Don't minimize this. You earned that shit—you've been so good to her. Glory in it."

"Yeah, but dude, let's get serious. She literally could be with anyone. I gotta be real about this. Maybe not read too much into what happened and move slow."

"Holy shit, are you sure you didn't talk to Lexi?"

"No. Whaddya talking about, Lexi?"

I paused for a second, wondering whether I wanted to get into this now. Then, becoming annoyed, I said, "It's just Lexi and I were talking today, and she needs to move slow too."

"That sounds bad. She didn't lay that 'it's not you, it's me' line on you, did she?"

"No, we sort of decided that we're down and . . ."

"Wait . . . down? What does that mean?"

"Um, um . . . A certain word beginning with the letter *L* came up today."

"Hmm, so my first guess would be *loser*, but that doesn't fit with the down part. Lube? Latex? Little?" he said, making the universal sign for a small penis with thumb and forefinger.

"Ha. Kiss my ass, house elf."

"Okay, okay. So what happened and why do you have to move slow?"

"You know that white dude with the afro, Ted Groman?"

"Always in the Big Star tee?"

"Yeah, him. They went out and Lexi got crushed when they broke up, so she wants to keep our shit all Zen and not use the *love* word."

"That doesn't sound so unreasonable. It's just a stupid word."

"Yeah, but why do I have to carry water for Groman?"

"Lexi had a bad experience and that Groman kid was part of it. You're not carrying water for him."

"Wow, you're taking her side? You're my friend—rage a little with me against this Groman fuck."

"Okay," he said in a tough Durden voice, "fuck Groman and his white man's fro. That is one low-frequency motherfucker with a poofy Bob Ross head. And what's with those Big Star tees? Like anybody besides us knows who that band is, and we're losers. How's that? You feel better now?"

"You're such an asshole," I said, laughing. "And yes, I get it. But goddammit, I want to be mad."

"Dude, what's to be mad about? Lexi is insanely hot, cool, and smart, and for some unknown reason she's in love with your sorry ass."

After thinking it over for a second, I did feel kind of dumb. "You're right. She is those things, and I'm pretty lucky to be with her."

"Maybe you shouldn't minimize either. You've been good to her too."

"Turning my words against me."

"Maybe the both of us should just make the most of this while we have the chance."

He was making sense and I said, "You're probably right. But there's something else too."

I explained that not only was Lexi wary of the *love* word, but she also was afraid the relationship would be doomed, like it was with Groman, because we both came from such shitty homes and had zero experience in dealing with all the emotions that came with being in love.

"Wow, that's a pretty astute observation."

"I know, right . . . It's blowing my mind."

"Still, she did give you some idea on a way forward."

"Yeah, like I know what to do."

"Don't undercut yourself. Just take the cues she gives you. She might be selling herself short too since she's been through it already."

"I don't know, man. It was such a great day and I was feeling so good about all of us and it ends with this car crash."

"Car crash? That's a bit much, snowflake."

"So I'm supposed to just sit back and let my girlfriend lead me around like I'm a dog on a leash?"

"Man, you are full of negative shit. Instead of thinking about it as being led around, maybe think about it as taking cues from her."

"There you go with *cues* again. Now who sounds like a snow-flake?"

"Okay, frame it in that prideful, negative way just like your old man would. See how that works for you."

Wow . . . shot landed. But rather than making me mad, like earlier with Lexi, it was another moment of recognition of who I was and what I was up against. "How'd you get so smart about this shit?"

"It's not about being smart. Listen to what she tells you, and try not to let your bullshit get in the way."

"It's that easy?"

"I don't know if it's easy, but at least you have a bit of a road map, which is way more than I have with Syd."

Sitting there, we talked more about the challenges confronting both of us with Syd and Lexi. I wasn't sure which situation was better, mine on the cusp of becoming serious or his with the excite-ment that comes with a beginning. Either way, I decided these were good problems to have and this was a good place to be on the first day of summer.

Just before I left, with my head whirling in fifty different direc-tions, he posed one last question. "So, dude, it's summer and we have plenty of time now. When are we going to kick over the parking cones on the Avenue?"

This I was not confused about. "Never. I told you I'm done with that shit."

"But I've gotten so much better on the bike. It'll be a breeze."

He'd worked his way up to almost being able to bunny hop, but was still a long way from being good, and I said, "You got a girl to worry about now. Forget about the goddamn parking cones."

"Yeah, you're right," he said, nodding. Though he seemed to agree with me, I had the distinct feeling he was just leaving it here for the moment and was going to come back at it later. Captain McDougal, always playing the long game.

CHAPTER 10

As much as McDougal constantly amazed me and defied all kinds of odds, the negative side of me was sure Syd was going to find a nice way *not* to be with him. Sidestepping it, she'd go cliché monster on him and say, "It's not you, it's me," and tell him she was just looking for something else. To her credit, though, they unofficially started to hang out as boyfriend and girlfriend. That meant, in addition to doing stuff with us like hanging at The Spot, going to the movies, and concerts at Canalside, during the day McDougal would become a pseudo big/little brother with Syd while she watched her stepsiblings. But it wasn't only her stepsiblings who took to him—he also ingratiated himself to her parents with his nerdy skills and charm, reformatting an old laptop and juicing up an ancient desktop with a couple of sticks of RAM. He also hooked them up with a router he wasn't using anymore, which brought the joy of Wi-Fi to her family.

In a teasing but nice kind of way, Syd told us that her mom was always making comments about how nice it was to be around a young man with so much on the ball, who had thoughts beyond his next tattoo. Then she'd imitate her saying, "Sydney, I know you're young, but that James, he's a keeper," which turned his face red with embarrassment.

Of course, this thrilled us beyond belief. "Lexi, I think you should go out with James too—he's a keeper."

"Yes, and you too, Jackson. We should all go out with James—he's so on the ball and a keeper."

"You guys are such jerks," he said, laughing.

Despite the unofficial dating status, however, Syd made it perfectly clear that what happened at The Spot on the last day of school was an aberration and any and all hand action was suspended until further notice, which was fine with McDougal. With this thing really happening between them, he was having a hard-enough time keeping his feet on the ground and was happy, for the time being, not to feel the pressure of sex. When I asked him how he was dealing with it after being so close that first time, he rolled his eyes and said, "Whaddya think?" and then made the universal gesture with his hand for rolling his own dice.

I was a little envious of McDougal for having such concrete guidelines with Syd, since my situation with Lexi was pretty confusing. Things were really good between us, and I felt closer to her than ever. And unlike McDougal's situation, where his hands were on lockdown, the upgrade in my relationship with Lexi came with a certain freedom to explore each other's bodies. This was beyond great, but I think I would have gone back into lockdown in exchange for the chance to express my feelings to her. Like she had warned, the step forward between us ignited an unwieldy burst of emotion, and being muzzled was way more stifling than I would have ever imagined. At one point, waiting for McDougal on his porch to get home from Syd's, I said to her, "It was probably a mistake to put a name to any of this. I should have just rolled with it and kept my mouth shut."

Optimistically she said, "I think we're doing fine. I really appreciate your patience."

"Yeah, but part of me always feels like this is a giant game of hot lava."

"That if you misstep you'll die a horrible death in a sea of boiling molten lava?"

"When you say it like that it sounds crazy, but you know what I mean," I said, laughing.

"Yes," she said, moving her arms under mine while looking up at me with those sparkling blue eyes. "I know what you mean. It'll get easier." She lingered there, just looking at me, almost as if her eyes were communicating what her voice wouldn't. She kissed me deeply and moved her hands all over my back. It was really great, but when we disengaged and didn't say anything, I had this incomplete feeling, like I was in the middle of constructing a story that was abruptly cut short before it was finished.

I did my best to roll with it and found solace in a summer that was just revving up. There were a lot of great shows coming up, but before we got to them, the next night we had to endure Twenty One Pilots at Canalside. To me TOP was a lame, suburbanized version of Eminem and their success was annoying. Lexi and McDougal tended to agree with me, but Syd liked them, called them a "guilty pleasure," and thought it would be fun to go down there and hang outside the venue and listen, since the show had been sold out for months and we didn't have tickets.

So we climbed into Lexi's mom's rusting Cherokee and in the ten-minute ride to Canalside, she smoked two menthols and told us the last real concert she went to was Dylan and the Dead back when the New Era Field was Rich Stadium in the late '80s. She had Lexi's eyes and was fun, recalling how she didn't really like Dylan or the Dead, but there was this guy . . . Lexi kept rolling her eyes, and after exiting the car, she said, "Thank god, we're Ubering it home."

"I don't know," McDougal said. "I like your mom. She's spunky."

A little annoyed, Lexi said, "She was just showing off."

On the way to the venue at Canalside, we walked past the *Little Rock* and the *Sullivan*, World War II-era ships permanently docked at Buffalo's naval park. In my plain black T-shirt, cutoffs, and Vans, I felt out of place walking among bearded hipsters in straw fedoras and flea-market American Eagle tees striding along with their pretty dates in flowery sundresses. There also seemed to be a preponderance of young ladies in high school letterman sweaters. I sort of understood the beard thing, but the letterman sweaters were a real curiosity, since it was obvious none of these girls ever made a team in their lives. They seemed so inauthentic, and I said to no one in particular, "All these fuckers think they're going to a rock show."

Syd definitely wasn't inauthentic, looking pretty badass in a cut-off Nirvana T-shirt, her eyes bold with black edging. "You're such a snob, Jackson."

Not expecting this pushback, I smiled and said, "Sorry, Sydney, there's rules and this is bullshit."

"Really . . . rules? Who makes these rules?" she asked.

"Chuck Berry, Pete Townshend, Patti Smith, Paul Westerberg, Liz Phair, Mitski . . . Artists who elevate the human experience."

"Really, they elevate the human experience? Everything doesn't have to be that . . . Ever hear of guilty pleasure, J-man?"

"Yes . . . Real Estate, Day Wave, Tennis. Those dream pop bands are guilty pleasures. This is bullshit."

Coming up on a vendor on the edge of the walkway, Lexi turned to Syd and said, "I'll get him to shut up. Jackson, please buy me a water."

A little taken aback, I raised my eyebrow at her. She raised her brow back at me, smiled, and said, "Please." Of course, there was no way to fight that smile off. McDougal bought Syd one too.

But after I dropped a five on a water, my disgust returned. "Five fucking dollars. These little Eminem impersonators are gentrifying water."

"You don't even know what *gentrify* means, dumbass," McDougal offered.

"I know at Woodstock both the water and brown acid were free. I know it didn't cost a cent to get spit on at an Iggy Pop show. I know in a few weeks we'll be right up front for free, rocking out at the Frank Turner show."

"Wait, gentrify? What's that?" Syd asked.

"It's this thing where rich people will overpay for a house in a poor neighborhood, then more rich people follow, buying up all the houses until the neighborhood eventually becomes too expensive for the poor people to live there," Lexi said.

"Exactly," McDougal said.

"I watch *Shameless*," Lexi said with a smile.

"Ah, I get it," Syd said. Then she turned to me and, raising her voice, said, "Jackson, whaddya talking about? The water is five fucking bucks at all these shows, even the free Frank Turner show."

Her response was a little much and I said, "Easy, Syd, I'm *mostly* kidding."

But she wasn't having it and quietly brooded next to McDougal, sipping her water. As much as we seemed to get along at times, like at The Spot the day before, there was an unstated rift between us. I think she held the shit with my old man against me, which was completely reasonable. For me, I was protective of McDougal and still got angry remembering how she laughed when Lexi had mentioned the idea of romance between them. I mean, she was just this hot little neighborhood girl fast-tracking the same mistakes her mom made, but with tatted motorcycle dudes.

I was self-aware enough to realize for me to judge anyone, given my humble origins, was a stretch. Shit, if my old man didn't outright catcall her, at the very least he had been checking her out for years, which was beyond creepy. And the thought of me having the nerve to judge her probably pissed her off—I know it would've pissed me off.

But Syd's bullshit was right there in front of us, even at Twenty One Pilots. McDougal and I hit the port-a-johns, and when we came back she was talking to some older dudes. Lexi was kind of off to the side with a less-than-encouraging face, while Syd had a big smile and playfully punched one of the dudes on the arm. McDougal wasn't blind to it, but he played it cool. After this happened a few more times in the following weeks, I asked if it pissed him off and he said, "I have to focus on my own shit. You see how hot she is—guys are going to talk to her. I can't stop that. All I can do is be me and if that ain't good enough, that's on her."

"I hate it when you're all sensible. Next time, let's mess those fuckers up."

"Yeah," he said sarcastically, "that's how I'll keep her interested."

"What if it's just me?"

"Especially if it's just you."

"C'mon, it'll be fun."

He gave me a look that let me know the conversation was over. I wasn't sure and he wasn't giving it away, but this shit with Syd seemed to bug me more than him. Or maybe he was just that cool and could float above it. That was my guess.

He certainly was cool in the eyes of Syd's stepsiblings. Lexi and I went with them to Caz Park one morning, and it was very obvious those kids did not get out much. Ten-year-old Cody and eight-year-old Carra sucked at everything. They didn't know how to climb a jungle gym, slide down a slide, or skip rocks. They were terrible at freeze tag and really easy to find playing hide-and-go-seek. I was surprised at how much fun I had and the joy I derived from teaching Cody, after like a hundred throws, to skip a rock across the creek.

Lexi whispered in my ear, "I like you like this. You'd be a good father."

I just looked at her and thought to myself . . . *Father?* Some of the best memories of my mom were here at Caz Park, and I really had to stay in the moment; otherwise, I would have gotten sad or angry. I was getting through it just fine until Lexi's comment, which made me angry, but not with my absent mother. I was angry with my old man. Helping Cody get up the jungle gym and use the slide was great, but when he finally skipped a rock after a hundred tries, it felt like a real accomplishment not only for him, but for me too, and I got mad 'cause I never had this with the old man.

With Lexi next to me, sitting on the bank of the creek, I quietly brooded as Cody continued to skip rocks. Attuned to my moods, she asked, "What's up? Why so quiet?"

Shot-putting a rock into the water, I said, "Why couldn't he ever do this with me? It's so fun."

"Your father?"

I nodded.

"Well, if he's anything like my dad, when he broke it off with my mom, he more or less broke it off with me and my brother too."

"I have like zero good memories of the fucking guy."

Looking away, she said, "Maybe that's not so bad. I have a couple of memories, one especially from when I was like ten. We were sitting on my cousin's porch and he was talking to me, telling me he loves me and that I'm his special girl and I'm going to grow up into a special lady. Just all this really nice stuff."

"Why is that so bad?"

"'Cause it was all bullshit and I fell for it," she said, her voice tinged with anger.

I sidled up closer, put my arm around her, and kissed her on the temple. Coming out of the kiss I was going to tell her she was my *special girl* but thought better of it. Instead, I tried to say it with my eyes and then kissed her again. It occurred to me staring at her sad, beautiful face that love had been unkind to her, not only with old boyfriends like Groman, but in general. And, all of a sudden I just kind of blurted out, "Lexi, I know I'm not supposed to say this and I know we may not last forever, but your old man was right, you are a special lady, and right here, right now, with every molecule of my being, I love you."

It felt really good to say it, but Lexi kind of just smiled, got up, and walked up the downward slanting bank over to the wading pool where McDougal, Syd, and Carra had their feet in the water. She was quiet for the rest of the day. When I texted her later, all I got was a bunch of one-word answers.

Knowing my mistake, I accepted Lexi's distance. It extended to McDougal's birthday party the next day, which a ton of people showed up to and was great fun. Denny and Mike (plus his wife) and some other scraggly-bearded gamers from Prince's came and were in total awe of McDougal, who was making the rounds with Syd at his side. Our extreme-biking friends Skeezy and JuJu were there. Some kids from his advanced classes showed up too and so did the art teacher, Mr. Fundalinski, who Sydney was on a first-name basis with: "Oh, hello, Martin." There were also some cousins, his uncomfortable and sober dad, and his mom's parents, the Hannons, who McDougal especially wanted me to meet.

Recently up from Florida for the rest of the summer, his grandmother was a petite woman attired as if she just came from a golf club, while his grandfather was this huge guy with a flattop and concrete hands. After McDougal introduced me as his best friend, his ex-military grandfather set out to test me right away. Crushing the bones in my hand while we shook, he said, "Hillary or Trump?"

"Bernie."

"Bernie," he said with a broad smile. "How's he going to pay for all his programs?"

"He's going to tax rich guys who live in Florida," I said.

"Good one, Jackson," he said with a laugh and then slapped me on the shoulder, but he didn't remove his hand, and nodding at my shoulder, he said, "Genetic or did you earn those?"

"P90X, sir."

"The workout my daughter does?"

"It's pretty tough, sir."

"How about the neighborhood police, Jackson? Are they tough on a kid like you?"

"Henry, stop interrogating him," McDougal's grandmother said with a shake of her head.

"It's okay, Mrs. Hannon. I don't mind." Then, looking up at McDougal's grandfather, I said, "I've been a black kid living in white neighborhoods my whole life, and from a very young age I was taught the proper way to act and talk to the police."

"Meaning?"

"I look them in the eye and answer their questions respectfully."

"Ah, good man. Do they single you out?"

"Henry," McDougal's grandmother said, growing increasingly frustrated.

"Mrs. Hannon, it's okay, really. Yes, when I first moved here about a year ago I got stopped a few times, but it wasn't a big deal. Like I said, I just answer their questions respectfully and we have no problems." For a brief second, I was going to say, "Except for this one time when I got caught kicking over parking cones and was brought home to my crazy old man . . ." but I was able to stop myself before making that mistake.

"Does it make you angry, Jackson?"

"Quite honestly, sir, yes it does. Just the other day I was walking down the street with my girlfriend"—and I nodded over to where Lexi was standing—"and this officer, who was new to the neighborhood or at least I never saw him before, stopped me for no reason and asked me where I lived, what I was doing, and how did I know this girl? It's one thing to stop me, but in front of my girlfriend, it was humiliating."

"I'm sorry for that, son. I'd be mad too."

"Thank you, sir. To be honest, it's not so bad. But sometimes when I'm walking down the street with Lexi, I get some pretty nasty looks—mostly from older people, no disrespect."

"None taken. One of the best things about my military career was the broad array of people I got to work with and had to depend on. We should all mix and work together like we do in the military.

The country would have a lot less problems. Ever think about the military, Jackson?"

"No sir, not really. I've only recently started thinking about college."

"College? How are you going to pay for college?"

"Like I said, Bernie is going to tax rich guys who live in Florida."

With that both he and his wife let out a big laugh, and he slapped me on the shoulder again. "I like you, Jackson. Where'd you find this guy, James?" he rhetorically asked McDougal, who had also been listening.

McDougal recounted how we met in that transition hallway and the events that followed with McManus, which got another big laugh.

Our conversation with McDougal's grandparents seemed to end at the same time as Syd and Lexi's discussion with Mr. Fundalinski, and we went to the part of the driveway where they were standing and told them about his grandparents and the Bernie stuff I'd said. Syd laughed, but Lexi remained stone-faced and said, "I know, I have eyes. I saw you laughing."

Her attitude, which continued through the night, was starting to grate on me. After eating some pizza and wings and before "Purple Rain" and "Born to Run" were destroyed on the rented karaoke machine, people were given the opportunity to say something about McDougal. Mike from Prince's Blade Gaming made a weird declaration about the respect the gaming community had for James. Skeezy said he looked forward to biking down the Avenue kicking over the parking cones with McDougal, which nobody but a few of us understood. His mom said how proud she was of the young man he was becoming and with a tear in her eye recounted an incident from third grade where McDougal was reprimanded at school for telling someone to "piss off." He was told that he couldn't speak to others with an angry tone or using curse words, he responded, "Piss? . . . Piss is not a curse word. I read it in *Harry Potter and the Order of the Phoenix.*" Everybody laughed except Lexi. She didn't laugh when I described McDougal's stars-and-stripes Toby Keith biking helmet either, which he later turned into a BMX Batman helmet and debuted in front of her and Syd while wearing a cape.

She was still quiet walking home, and when we got to her house, I asked, "Are we breaking up, Lexi?"

"I don't know. Are you going to keep saying things I asked you not to say?"

"You're kidding, right? I told you how special you are and that I love you, and now you're torturing me with it."

"Doesn't matter that what you said was nice or that you had good intentions. I opened up to you and told you how those words hurt me in the past and asked that we go slow, and you just blew it off."

"Blew it off? It's been a month and I haven't said a word."

Unimpressed, she just gave me a long disapproving look. I stomped off, cursing to myself that this was total bullshit, but by the time I sat on the bench at the library across from my street, I had calmed down. I thought about how Lexi asked me to think about the *love* word from her point of view and the more I turned it over in my head I grudgingly had to admit she was right. As well intentioned as I was, I crossed a line she had asked me not to cross. And as I continued to sit there, it also occurred to me that in a completely unironic way, the word *love* was wreaking havoc in our relationship just as it had done before with her and Groman.

CHAPTER 11

AFTER MY REVELATION, I sent Lexi a text wholeheartedly acknowledging she had been right about the *love* word. I surrendered to the fact that it was indeed causing us misery and told her I would do my best to keep my mouth and emotions in check.

She called me and said, "Thank you. Sorry for overreacting. I want this to work, but it's hard and I'm learning how to do this too. If we go slow, it'll be all right."

It continued to be tough but tolerable. It was also weird to me that though we couldn't really talk about our future together, one hot day sitting in shade against the abandoned plant back at The Spot, she asked me in a real serious way what my plans were after high school.

"Whaddya mean 'after high school'? I don't know what I'm doing later today."

"Jackson," she said, tilting her head thoughtfully, letting me know she wanted a serious answer.

"I don't know. College, hopefully."

"You know New York State has this free college tuition program they're taking up? It's called the Excelsior Program."

"Oh yeah, I know about Excelsior. Just before the old man went back to work this spring, our cable got cut and they were talking about it all the time on local radio. The dumb ass didn't get how stupid he sounded complaining about his tax money going to lazy ass millennials when he had been on the dole all winter. He hates Governor Cuomo almost as much as he hates Hillary."

"What a surprise, but if it goes through, it'll be great for us."

"I guess, but it seems like one of those pie-in-the-sky, too-good-to-be-true things."

"If it happens, I could go to SUNY Albany and get my public administration degree."

"What's that?"

"It's a public sector job, like with the government."

"How do you already know you want to do that?"

"There was this girl who graduated from South Park that has a PA degree and works for the state legislature. She gave a presentation in one of my classes."

"Is she one of those staffers sitting behind politicians on TV, whispering in their ear or handing them papers during hearings? That doesn't look like so much fun to me."

"No, but you could be one of those staffers. She works for the legislature doing research. Like this past year when the state was considering funding for the New York City subway, she went into the bowels of the subway, got a tour, talked to engineers and found out what upgrades were needed, presented the information to the legislature, and then oversaw the bidding process."

The way Lexi was talking reminded me of that really together girl I met at the Erie County Home, Jessica Lee, who was doing a gerontology masters in social work. She went on about trying to get some money together to dorm so she wouldn't be so in debt and talked about this loan forgiveness program that you could use if you worked in the public sector for ten years.

"If they pass this Excelsior thing and I get ten grand together, maybe I'll only be twenty or thirty in debt, which would be a breeze to pay off," she said confidently.

"I know some kids get way more in debt, but thirty still sounds like a lot to me."

"Not when you're making sixty or seventy. It's very manageable."

It was a bit odd to me that Lexi had so thought through all of this, yet crumbled when I told her I loved her. It flashed through my mind to point this out, but the insanity of the thought only lasted a brief moment and exited my head at warp speed. But I wondered, as she continued to talk about the future and getting the hell out of here, if love was more about what you didn't say than what you did say. In our case that seemed to be true, and it bugged me, and again for a brief, insane second, I thought about bringing it up, but moved on instead.

Ironically enough, in the coming days my old man would present an opportunity that would get Lexi's college fund going. For the year I lived with him and before, half of our roof on Lockwood was covered by a tarp. The city had cited us several times and now was on the verge of imposing fines unless we fixed it. After screaming about it for several days, my old man found a roofing side job a few blocks over on Ladner Street. Apparently, our little slice of South Buffalo was becoming the subject of gentrification, 'cause the old man swindled ten grand from "some fuckhead in a Beemer," as he called him, for a tear-off and replacement on a small ranch, which was twice what the job was really worth. Materials for the ranch and our house totaled six grand, and the old man said he would split the remaining four with me as long as I got some friends to help. If we worked hard we could get both jobs done over two weekends. I asked Skeezy, JuJu, Mike, and Denny, but nobody except Lexi and McDougal really considered it. Despite the money and because of my old man Syd wanted no part of it. Lexi thought long and hard about it before eventually coming on board.

McDougal's mom was all for some hard work, but after learning we had no insurance, she said James could help with the cleanup, but under no circumstances was he to climb up or down any ladders.

The old man was skeptical when I was only able to enlist McDougal and Lexi, but we got after it. It was really hard work and it took a few hours to toughen up our hands and asses as we sat with roofing shovels, tearing into and removing the old shingles. Even with an extra blast of cortisone McDougal had to rest often, and Lexi would pick up the slack of throwing the old shingles into the rented dumpster. While the old man knew exactly what to do, he needed to take breaks in the hot sun too.

After not saying much all day beyond giving us some basic instructions, he seemed happy with what we'd accomplished, tearing the old roof off and getting the ice shield and felt paper down. There was some cleanup left to do, but with a half-smile he said, "This was a good day's work. We'll get that tomorrow."

He warned us that we would be sore in the morning. And holy shit, was he right. He woke me up just before 6 a.m. and told me he was going to Home Depot for some materials and then was going to work on the drip edge, and we should meet him at the house no later than 8 a.m. He also said, "Text your friends and tell them to get a good stretch because there's more hard work ahead."

He was so right about the need to stretch. Sluggish and sore,

I felt like a freight train had not only hit me, but also stopped and backed over me a few times.

Lexi responded with, *Arrgh!*

McDougal's return text was, *Goddamn, I'm dying.*

The stretching did help to a point, loosening up my shoulders and hammies, but my hands and ass, those hurts could not be helped with stretching.

Seeing our pain and listlessness, the old man smiled as he gave out directions. He was going to put down the first layer of shingles around the perimeter using the nail gun while we got the bundles of shingles up onto the roof. McDougal would bring them to me from the truck, and I would run them up the ladder, and then Lexi would position them around the roof. It took a little time to get used to the weight of sixty-pound bundles of shingles and the right way to move them, but after some trial and error we found a good rhythm.

Breathing heavily as he handed the shingles off to me, McDougal was really funny saying stuff like, "I should've studied harder when I was in school; I should've done more cardio in my twenties; I should've switched to non-filters; I should've dropped the gluten from my diet. But what I really should've done, like yesterday, was become a ninja, so I could kick your ass for talking me into doing this bullshit."

He was hilarious, which made the pain of carrying those sixty-pound bundles up the ladder more bearable. The fact that the old man let us listen to our tunes instead of classic rock also made the job more acceptable. He even liked a song by Wilco, which prompted McDougal to dial up an alt-country radio station on his phone. Stuff by Son Volt, Shelby Lynn, Drive-By Truckers. He loved a heavy guitar song by Slobberbone called "Gimmie Back My Dog," where a guy complained about an ex taking his dog after they broke up. "That's good stuff," the old man said with a smile.

Once we had fifteen bundles on the roof, the old man would work by himself with the nail gun, while Lexi and I would put down shingles at a much slower pace using an old-school hammer and nails as McDougal continued the cleanup. It was a good system and McDougal could probably get ten bundles to me at the bottom of the ladder before he bombed out and needed a little break.

We had everything pretty much sewn up by late Sunday afternoon and would only have to come back the next day to rehang a couple of gutters. Now that we had some experience and our hands and asses were all toughened up, we did even better the next weekend, even though there were two roofs to tear off on our house.

While paying us, the old man said, "I thought we were undermanned. But you did good. I could run a crew with you guys."

It was a nice, heartfelt thing that he said, but later, with a few beers in him, he asked if I wanted to do more of these side jobs, then got mad when I said I wanted to think about it a little before committing, which prompted him to say, ". . . Lazy fucking millennial."

McDougal refused any money, saying he was all set with cash and that Lexi and I should just split it. When we told him this was totally unacceptable, he agreed to let us take him and Syd to the Florence and the Machine show at Six Flags the weekend after school started. This was not ideal, but he insisted and grudgingly we said okay to his generous ass.

As good as the roofing experience was for gaining a bit of respect from the old man and for my bottom line, it probably contributed to the passing of my grandmother. The old man came into my room in the middle of the night the following Thursday and said, "The Home just called—your grandmother is sick. Let's go."

"Wait . . . what?" I said, my head fuzzy with sleep.

"We need to get to the Home, ASAP . . . Your grandmother is sick."

"How bad?"

"What do you think, if they're calling now. Let's go."

We got a couple of coffees at the twenty-four-hour Tim Horton's on Orchard Park Road and didn't say a word to each other the entire thirty-minute ride. Instead, we listened to some crazy radio show turned way down low called Coast to Coast that talked all this dumb shit about aliens building the Egyptian pyramids. I was happy for the distraction, though, because my head was racing as I tried to convince myself what was happening, really wasn't happening. I mean, the old man said she was sick, but since the stroke she more or less was always sick, so it was just the same old, same old. But this middle-of-the-night trek made it hard to keep the delusion going, and pessimistically, I gave into the reality of what was happening. I realized too, I was not ready for this and felt really stupid for not ever thinking about this inevitability.

When we got there, she wasn't in her usual room, which she shared with some hard-looking woman of Eastern European descent. The kindly head nurse directed us to another room, where she was hooked up to a breathing machine. She told us my grandmother had a chest infection and was aspirating, but the larger issue was she seemed to be giving up. She mentioned the last two weekends we didn't visit were very disorienting for her, which kind of shocked me. I thought our Sunday visits were always an obligatory kind of penance for the old man, one of the few he followed through on. I never thought about her potentially getting something from them or how our absence would negatively affect her. It was another moment of revelation, and I felt bad that all my beautiful, kind grandmother had in this world was me and Mickey Wolf.

I was sitting at my grandmother's side, holding her hand in the darkened room, listening to the methodic hum of the breathing machine and wishing she could somehow acknowledge my presence, when a young female doctor entered the room. I only heard a few words—hospital, feeding tube—but the old man strongly shook his head *no* to everything she said.

We were ushered out of the room to the empty sitting area with the glass ceilings, and the old man spoke his first words to me since back at the house. "Settle in. It's going to be a while."

If you tried real hard, you could feel the hominess of that darkened little sitting area. Small centerpieces sat on glass tables that were flanked by a mix of real and fake plants, producing a sort of oasis in the middle of the facility, which otherwise was so cold and dreary. You couldn't quite escape the scent of urine, but a calming hum that was occasionally interrupted by the yell of a distressed resident or a staff member walking by filled the air, and a comfortable wistfulness came over me as I sat on one end of the couch and the old man sat on the other end.

After dozing a bit, I was awoken by the morning bustle of the shift changing. Over at the reception desk, Jessica Lee was talking to a woman who had some brochures. They looked over at us and, seeing I was awake, started coming toward us. The old man was still dozing, and I reached across and nudged him awake.

Extending her hand to me and then the old man, Jessica introduced herself and Sue Miller, the woman with the brochures, who was from Hospice. With an astute kindness, Jessica said she was sorry for this turn in my grandmother's health and Ms. Miller could help us as we moved forward in this process. Jessica also said she would be here all day if we needed anything. Again, I was struck by her competence, which came in the form of warmth this time.

The interaction with Ms. Miller was short and to the point. In mid-sentence, after being told just a few things about palliative care, the old man got up, went outside, and had a smoke. After she finished telling me about some things to expect going forward, I thanked her and instead of telling her that my old man was a rude asshole, I made some shit up about him having a tough time. She smiled and told me not to worry about it, then gave me some brochures and said my grandmother's hospice room would be ready shortly.

The room was nice only because it was private. There was some fake hardwood flooring, a couple of stiff loveseats, and a small table with a couple of chairs. A window cloudy with age looked out at the other side of the building across that little courtyard where we sat in the spring. I took one of the chairs and sat next to the bed, holding my grandmother's hand, while the old man positioned himself on one of the loveseats and fiddled with the remote that controlled the TV perched on the wall.

Removed from the breathing machine and feeding tube, she seemed more human curled up in a ball on the bed. She was still far from herself and had been since the stroke, but at least now, as compromised and fragile as she was, she was going to meet her fate with dignity. Though I still couldn't bring myself to fully accept what was happening and didn't understand what was going on with the old man, who sat there so disinterested looking up at the TV, I was glad for his stand about removing her from those machines.

At any rate, as a strange little gurgle accompanied her rhythmic breathing, I decided I wasn't going to waste my time figuring out what was going on with the old man. Instead, I was going to try and remember things about her and our life together. And as I sat there for the next several hours holding her hand and looking at her broken-down seventy-one-year-old body, a bunch of ordinary things from the past ran through my head. I remembered her getting angry if she had to call me in twice to eat when I was playing street hockey, and us drinking hot chocolate after we shoveled the snowy driveway, and her endlessly telling me to turn the music down. But most vivid were the memories of the way she used to try and comfort my absent mom and the no-nonsense approach she had with my old man. She was also no-nonsense with me, but it was always done in a way to appeal to my better self. If I left my clothes on the bathroom floor or got in trouble at school, with a cigarette dangling from the side of her mouth, she would give me this fierce look that let me know I was better than what I was showing and she was not going to put up with it. I hated to disappoint her, and sitting there thinking about this, I laughed to myself and out loud said, "I love you, Grandma." Though I wasn't expecting it, she squeezed my hand ever so slightly, which made me happy and filled me with a renewed hope.

Just then, Louise, a nurse's aide who'd worked with my grandmother since she'd been admitted to the Home, came into the room. She expressed her regret for my grandmother's failing health, sort of fluffed her pillow, and asked if we had any questions or needed anything. I looked at the old man, who remained focused on the

TV, and said no. But as she was leaving, I thought of something and said, "Yeah, hold on, what is that gurgling sound she's making?"

"You have a phone?" she asked.

Actually, I did. After the roofing job, McDougal gave me one of his old iPhones and added me to his family plan. He wanted sixty bucks to cover the line fees for a few months, thinking that's how long it would take for his mom to forget I was on the plan and would just pay it. I nodded and said, "Yes."

She said, "Look on Google at *rattle* and *illness*. That will explain it," and then smiled sympathetically before leaving the room.

I did the search and the first entry was a Wikipedia page: *Death rattle*. It explained, *Death rattles are sounds often produced by someone who is near death as a result of fluids such as saliva and bronchial secretions accumulating in the throat and upper chest. Those who are dying may lose their ability to swallow and have increased production of . . .* I didn't need to read on as the temporary elation of my grandmother squeezing my hand a few minutes earlier came to a grinding halt. I got up from my chair and started walking aimlessly through the halls. I ended up at the reception desk with Jessica Lee and, looking down at my phone, was going to explain to her the meaning of *death rattle*. But after getting two words out, I lost it and started to cry uncontrollably. She walked me to an empty conference room adjacent to the reception area and held my hand as I let it out.

When I was done several minutes later, I apologized for my lack of self-control.

With warmth and kindness she said, "Nothing to apologize for . . ."

She sat me down and went and got me a bottle of water and

some tissues and stayed with me. After a few minutes a strange sadness came over me, which in a weird way felt really good, really right. It was at that moment I fully accepted the inevitability of my grandmother's fate. I apologized again to Jessica and thanked her. She gave me a little half smile and nodded.

After I returned, the old man got up and said he was going to step out for a bit. While he was gone my grandmother's old friends Barb and Patty came into the room. There was some small talk where I found out the old man had called them and explained the situation, I relinquished my chair next to the bed, and both of them, with pained faces, said their goodbyes. Hearing them, I was again on the verge of losing it, but I mostly kept it together. Afterward I walked them out and thanked them. I also assured them we would be in touch when everything played out.

The old man came back a while later smelling like booze, and after I told him about Barb and Patty, he took his seat looking up at the TV and I took my spot bedside. Except for occasionally getting up to hit the vending machine and him stepping out for a smoke and a pull of whatever he was drinking, this was how we would remain for the next day as her rattle became staggered, but deeper and more pronounced. During the hours that rolled along blankly toward one inescapable ending, I fully embraced the weird, sad melancholy I was feeling. Then, almost anticlimactically, after hours and hours of staggered breathing, in the blue of the night she took one last giant gulping breath and was gone.

I sobbed quietly into my hands while the old man stood at the end of the bed. After a moment, he came and put his hand on my shoulder. This display of affection caught me a little of guard, but not as much as his lined ashen face wet with grief.

CHAPTER 12

THE WAKE AND funeral went by in a blur and left me exhausted. Lexi, McDougal, and Syd came for the whole night session of the wake and the funeral the next day. So did my grandmother's old friends Barb and Patty, who were better ambassadors at meeting and greeting people than the old man. He spent most of the wake out in the parking lot having beers with his buddies. McDougal's mom and his very awkward dad came, as did Jessica Lee, which thrilled me. She was a South Buffalo girl, and after she'd paid her respects she told me to take care with an air of finality, which made me realize since my grandmother was gone, I would probably never see her again. In a subdued panic I ran after her, and just as she was getting into a running Honda, I called out to her. She waited with the car door open, and when I got there I had no idea what to say to her without it sounding like some lame come-on. I looked into the car and she introduced me to some dude behind the wheel, who barely took his eyes off his phone. Trying to get on with it as I stood there stammering, she said, "Yes, Jackson?"

Finally, I just said, "You want to hang out sometime? I mean like friends or something."

Sensing my awkwardness, she smiled and held out her hand. "Give me your phone." As she was punching in her number, she asked if I liked coffee.

"Yeah, I can do a double double."

"Text me when things settle down. I know this little café-slash-bookstore on Abbott Road."

"I know that place. Words," I said, feeling like I'd just scored.

She got in the car, smiled, and waved as the driver pulled away. Caught up in the moment, I stood there and into my head came images of us at Words, drinking coffee from big ceramic mugs. She was telling me something, and I was enthralled not only with what she was saying, but also with her. As exciting as it was to muse about Jessica, doing so also came with some guilt. Lexi had been so great and supportive with all of my grandmother stuff, and I felt really close to her, but there I was with an undeniable, impossibly silly crush on Jessica Lee.

Lexi was waiting for me right inside the doors as I re-entered the funeral home. With a funny tone, she said, "What's her name again? And what was she doing with your phone?"

"Jessica Lee, from the Erie County Home. She was giving me her number. She's really smart. We can learn stuff from her."

"We?"

"Yes . . . we," I said, taking her hand. "You know how that girl who gave the presentation to your class about public administration inspired you? Jessica is like that. She's getting a masters in geriatric social work and really has her shit together."

"Wait . . . Geriatrics, isn't that old-people stuff? You wanna work with old people?"

"No. I have no idea what I want to do, besides hang out with you."

"Don't be funny, Jackson. So why meet with her?"

"She told me about her own grandmother, who came to a bad end because her family was unaware of the services available to her. As a result of that, Jessica is trying to make a difference for other people with this geriatric social work thing. I think it's pretty cool that she's using her career to right this wrong from her own life. Don't you?"

"Yeah, I guess."

I could tell Lexi was just blowing it off, but I couldn't get Jessica or a future without my grandmother out of my head. Her death had a greater effect on me than I might have imagined, filling me with a forlorn sense of life's fleeting nature. And, I also brooded about who I was and what I was supposed to do with my own life. Most profoundly, seeing and hearing the brutal way life slipped away from her, I suddenly stopped being mad at everyone: the old man, my absent mom, Syd, even rockhead McManus. I didn't understand it, but a few days after the funeral, as we were sitting in his garage, McDougal conjectured that it was my Buddha moment.

"My Buddha moment?" I asked.

"Yeah, ya know, Siddhartha . . . Buddha, you don't know the story?"

"I know the shit we learned in World History . . . The Eightfold Path, the release from suffering. Think they called it samsara?"

He got up, went into the house for a minute, and came back with a thin paperback by Hermann Hesse titled *Siddhartha*. He handed it to me and said, "The Buddha was born Siddhartha Gautama and was the son of a king. As a young prince he lived in a palace with giant walls and never saw the old, the sick, or the poor, until one day he went beyond the walls and saw an elderly man and then a decaying corpse. Distressed, he came upon a group of ascetics who promised him release, so he followed them."

Puffing up my chest, I said to McDougal, "I get that you see me as a prince, but I'm not sure about being an ascetic, at least not until I lose my virginity."

"Yeah, I'm not sure you get what the ascetics are about. And besides, once they see how you eat, they'd probably say no thanks."

"What? I can skip a few breakfasts."

"There's a little more to it than skipping some bacon sandwiches. It's like total self-denial and it didn't work for Siddhartha. He went his own way instead, and after some trial and error, he found release under the Bodhi tree and in the process founded one of the world's great religions."

"So what's my Buddha moment?"

"It's the shit you saw and went through with your grandmother."

I sat quietly for a moment, taking this in, and then asked, "Did you have a Buddha moment?"

"Since my pituitary bullshit and the stuff with my old man, my life has been an endless series of Buddha moments."

After another pause I said, "I don't get how seeing my grandmother die made me less angry."

"It didn't make you less angry. It cracked open the compassion buried inside of you."

"How?"

Shaking his head, he said, "You're really not smart, are you? Her death helped you see how fucked we all are, how we all come to this brutal end, and it made you feel compassion and mercy for others. For everyone."

Laughing, I said, "Kiss my ass, runt boy. I don't have any compassion for you."

"Yeah, I think you do, tough guy. I saw it that day you knocked me down outside of Rite Aid and felt bad."

"Whaddya mean, you saw it?"

"The fact that you didn't kick me or walk away let me know there was something to you. Something more. Probably something *good*."

I was still emotionally raw from the last few weeks, and the word *good* hit me hard and reminded me of that text McDougal sent the morning after the big fight with my old man outside of the bar. He quoted a song about a kid who struggles with a drunk, abusive father and refers to himself as "young and good." Like then, tears started to well in my eyes. I looked away and after a moment McDougal said, "You're good, Jackson. Believe it." He paused and then continued, "You're dumb as shit, but you're good."

We both laughed as the tears fell from my eyes. McDougal stood up, nudged my arm for me to stand, and then hugged me. Putting his head into my chest, he really hugged me. At first there was some awkwardness, but as McDougal held onto me it any weirdness just floated away.

In the weeks that followed as the summer came to an end, I brooded about all the people in my life: my old man, Lexi, Jessica. Freed from our Sunday obligation of going to the Home, the old man started to drink almost as soon as he got up. It was pretty obvious why McDougal's sad-sack old man produced Buddha moments and mine didn't, since my old man was an easy-to-hate prick. But I wasn't hating him these days and was making a conscious effort to avoid conflicts. I looked after myself and generally just kept my shit tight. As the tension between us evaporated, I also looked for opportunities where we could come together in a positive way, and on the Sunday morning before Labor Day, I talked him into going down to Gallagher Beach.

Gallagher Beach was at the foot of Tifft Street and butted up against long-abandoned grain silos that were part of Buffalo's past. These days it was the first leg of waterfront redevelopment that eventually led to Canalside downtown. Generally, it was a crappy little beach that used to be called Ghetto Beach before it was cleaned up. It was still kind of crappy, but now you could rent kayaks, launch a windsurfing rig, swim or just catch some rays.

On the multilevel retaining wall next to the beach we set up our cooler, and a little boombox between a couple of city issued Adirondack chairs facing the water. It was a breezy, warm day, and as the old man was tuning in the classic rock station on the boombox, I pulled out my iPhone and told him with Apple Music I had access to just about every Led Zeppelin song ever recorded. But instead of Zeppelin he wanted to hear some Slobberbone, which he remembered from the roofing job earlier in the summer.

As I dialed up a Slobberbone alt-country mix, he told me when he was a teenager he'd come down here, drink beers with his buddies, and jump out windows of the grain silos into the deep harbor water below.

"Some guys made it all the way to the seventh story, but I only made it to four."

Looking up, I couldn't imagine the fourth floor let alone the seventh. "Were you scared?"

"Hell yes." He laughed. "Every time. After doing the fourth floor a few times, I made my way up to five and stood there for like ten minutes while my friends egged me on. But I said, 'Fuck it, I'm done. Four is good enough.'"

"How many guys made it to seven?"

"Just a few except for this dude Lefty Wallace, who is in Attica or dead. He did it a lot, but seven was a one-off for most everybody else."

"What was with this Lefty guy?"

"He was this crazy fucker who pushed everything too far—drugs, booze, women. Ended up killing his wife."

"How?"

"He was messed up on angel dust or something and shot her," he said, his voice trailing off.

"Phenylethanol is today's angel dust." But the old man just looked out at the water and took a big pull on his Bud Light. With the roofing job and other side work he was doing on Ladner Street for the "Beemer fuckhead," it had been a prosperous summer and he was able to step it up with Bud Lights.

A mournful female voice came up in the mix and after a long pause, looking at my phone connected to the boombox, he finally asked, "Who's this?"

I wasn't sure and had to check the display. "Lucinda Williams, 'Are You All Right?'"

It was a simple question song with dreamy atmospherics. It possessed the old man.

"Man, I never heard a voice like that. You got more of her?" he asked, not really understanding how streaming worked.

"Yeah, I got everything."

"Play some more."

When I looked up after putting Lucinda into shuffle mode, he was holding out a Bud Light for me. I hesitated for a second, but took the beer, which made him smile. I opened it and we tapped cans and both of us said, "Cheers." Taking that first bitter sip, I cringed, and the old man laughed and said, "Nice face."

From there we settled back in our chairs and looked out at the water as the beautiful Lucinda Williams songs drifted out into the harbor like a siren song. I'd brought my copy of *The Sound and the Fury* and tried to read a few lines, but would forget them almost instantly because Lucinda was absolutely crushing me. The old man too. He just had this faraway look to him. At one point, during a song called "Sweet Old World," the music was so moving I had to fight back tears. It was all so peaceful and calm as we looked at the water, which was dotted with a few lazy kayaks and sailboats in the distance.

Of course, with my old man, our peaceful, hypnotic morning couldn't just fade away in beauty and wonder. It had to end with rage and the threat of violence. A big Hispanic family set up on the beach to the right of us and were loud. They weren't doing anything wrong; there was just a lot of them and they were noisy. He went off on them, telling them to "shut the fuck up" and to "go back to Mexico," but I got him to the truck before any punches were thrown. After he unloaded all his "spic" and "wetback" slurs in the truck and calmed down, I told him, "I had a good time this morning."

After a long pause, he replied, "Me too."

What wasn't such a good time was meeting Jessica Lee at Words with Lexi. After we settled into a little corner of the bookstore with our coffees and exchanged small-talk pleasantries, I explained my Buddha moment and my newfound compassion.

She laughed and said, "That's like the line in the Clash song 'Lost in the Supermarket' about how it's hard to see over a hedge in the suburbs."

I knew that song but not the line, and quickly pulled up the lyrics on my phone and got all tingly at the back of my neck reading them. "Wow," I said to Jessica, "that's the same thing. Ancient princes and '70s British punk bands dealing with the same issues."

"Like a South Buffalo kid who lost his grandmother."

Lexi was bored not only with this present conversation, but also with how I was going on and on about my newfound compassion. She thought, especially with my old man, the goodwill I was showing him was going to blow up in my face. I tried to explain that I wasn't looking for anything in return from him, that I was making the effort simply because it was the right thing to do.

Jessica, who was a more skilled communicator, put it in a way where both of us were correct. "Lexi is exactly right. If you have expectations of your father, you're going to be let down, but if you engage him without expectation and don't get dragged into his destructive world, you'll be fine."

"He's such an asshole," Lexi said.

Feeling defensive, I said, "Yeah, well, he's my asshole and I want to see this through. Why are you so against even trying?"

"I know how these things end."

Jessica, rightly sensing she was getting caught in the middle of our fight, got up and used the restroom.

Looking intently at Lexi, I said, "I know you're probably going to be right about all this, but I have to try. It's the right thing to do." But she just looked past me without saying a word.

When Jessica returned, she told us about her last internship this past spring with a human-services agency doing community outreach. This meant she worked with two other people identifying seniors who had received services from their agency in the past, but for one reason or another contact with them had lapsed. So, their job was to knock on doors and see what was happening with these people. And what they found was almost never good. Some had died, some were in financial peril, and some had lost the mental facility to make contact. They even found a lady who had been on her bedroom floor for like six hours with a broken hip, which in the long run turned out to be a good thing because after she had gotten therapy and healed up, she agreed to having a system installed that made it possible to get help if she was in trouble.

Lexi just sat there, half listening with this stone face. And god-damn if she wasn't right about my old man and his bullshit.

Earlier, before I had left to meet Jessica with Lexi, he was drinking beer, putting a new serpentine belt on the Ranger with his friend Del. When I got home he was on the living room floor, passed out next to an empty fifth of Black Velvet. As bad as the beer got at times, whiskey was absolute kryptonite. I cleaned up around him, putting the empty beer cans in the return bin. Then I went outside and got his toolbox that was still in the driveway and put it in the back hall. But while I was out there, Mrs. Hagan's new rescue dog spotted me and started barking from behind her fence. I made the situation worse by going over there to try to get the dog to stop, and Mrs. Hagan added more to it by coming out and trying to tell the dog I was the nice boy from next door who cut the grass. None of it worked and the dog continued to bark and bark and bark. After several minutes of this, the old man stormed out the front door and screamed, "Shut that fucking dog up!"

I went toward him with my arms extended and in a calming voice said, "Dad, Dad, Dad . . . It's okay," but when I got close, out of nowhere he headbutted me, knocking me momentarily dizzy. When I regained my composure, I locked him up and dragged him into the house as he continued to curse out the dog and Mrs. Hagan. Once inside, as gently as possible I took him to the ground. It wasn't long before he stopped struggling and was passed out again.

After untangling from him, I went to the mirror and there was a drop of blood just above my eyebrow where he headbutted me. But that was the least painful thing to come of this little dustup, which I was sure he wouldn't remember. After so much effort to make things right with the old man, I was really let down that he came after me, just like Lexi had predicted. Sitting back in a tattered living-room chair listening to him snore as little spit bubbles formed at the edges of his mouth, I didn't know what hurt more—the headbutt or the fact that Lexi was so right.

CHAPTER 13

WITH THE NEW school year not only was I challenged with harder classes and a bigger workload, but also my newfound empathy and compassion was severely tested and not just by the old man. As promised, Lexi and I took McDougal and Syd to the Florence and the Machine concert at Six Flags that first weekend after school started. Syd seemed distant the whole day, even during Courtney Barnett, who played a blistering, show-stealing opening set. This came after a week at school where on several occasions I saw her laughing and joking with some goth dudes. Well, maybe not laughing and joking, but smiling and looking somewhat bemused—they were goth dudes, after all. She even sat with them for half of lunch the day before the concert instead of with Lexi, me, and McDougal. I asked Lexi about it and she didn't think anything was up. McDougal tried to downplay it too, but added his usual line: "All I can do is be me and if that's not good enough, it's not good enough."

As it turned out, it wasn't good enough. A couple of days after the Florence show, Syd dumped him. He dropped the news on me back at The Spot after we'd worked a scam at South Park Liquor on the Avenue. McDougal had occupied the old dude working the counter with some bullshit about needing empty boxes to store his Star Wars Lego sets while I'd lifted a fifth of Jameson.

"She was nice about it," he said in a subdued voice. "Said she wasn't ready to have a steady boyfriend and that I was a great guy and any girl would be lucky to have me."

"That's true, ya know," I said, trying to be reassuring.

Looking away, he whispered, "But I don't want other girls. I want her."

Like he had done for me in the trying moments after the fight at Outlaws with the old man, I got up from my crate, nudged McDougal up, and drew him into me. Under a dreary, threatening sky he buried his head in my chest, and sobbed quietly. When he was all cried out, we sat back down and didn't say much of anything.

Taking little bitter pulls on the whiskey, we listened to his moody *Save Me* playlist, which had tunes by Kelley Ryan, Cat Power, Iron & Wine, and others. Searching for ways to somehow lessen his pain, I had the urge to lighten the mood with some jokes but thought better of it. Eventually, spurred on by the melancholic tunes, McDougal cracked, "God, you'd think in all this depressing shit I would've included an actual fucking suicide song."

"No Lana Del Rey on there? She makes me want to kill myself."

"Don't mess with Lana." He smiled.

We weren't able to sustain this breezy interlude and fell back into just listening to the music and talking a bit about how bad the whiskey tasted. After a while we gave up on it without really catching a buzz and went to his house. On the way I tried to call up some anger toward Syd, like before when she was so dismissive of the idea of dating McDougal, but it just wasn't there. Though I felt terrible for McDougal, I sort of could see why she did what she did and maybe even empathized with her.

Because she was always caring for her siblings, she wasn't able to hang much with us at The Spot or in McDougal's garage where we talked and laughed and grew. When the conversation turned to new bands, books, or apps, she wasn't there and was always playing catch-up. Our world moved fast with a lot of variables while she was stuck in the monotonous cycle of being a caregiver, and I sensed we made her feel insecure and a little dumb, even though McDougal fawned over her and was so patient catching her up. But it wasn't good enough.

Of course, where Syd didn't have to feel insecure or dumb, with her burnished red hair and fierce blue eyes, was every room where there were guys. Whether goth, biker, or douchebag Gary Clausen, dudes were drawn to her and desperate for her attention. We came with the baggage of curiosity and intelligence, especially McDougal. The irony was, had he been dumb and less charming, she would've never given him a second of her time.

At his house his mom had made a delicious chicken parm dinner. She knew something was up, but McDougal mostly stonewalled her. Later, the mood lightened when he looked over my AP Geometry homework. "Wow, second week of Geometry and you still know what you're doing. All those freshman girls must be impressed."

The class was indeed mostly populated with freshmen who had taken Algebra in eighth grade. I was a year behind because until freshman year, when I met my English teacher, Mr. Cummings, there was no one to challenge me academically, so I took the easy math.

Happy that we were joking, I quipped, "Of course. Those girls are trying to catch my eye, but I like the mature ladies like your mom."

He crumpled up a sheet of paper and threw it at me and then said, "Or Jessica."

"Jessica, whaddya talking about?"

"Dude, c'mon."

"C'mon what?"

"Really? You're really going to sit there and say you don't have a thing for Jessica?"

"Um . . . yeah," I said, making air quotes with my fingers, "I don't have a thing for Jessica. She's smart and has her shit together—that's it."

"Your moony-eyed face said something different at the wake, especially when you came back with her number . . . You were like my mom when she has a glass of wine and hears a Go-Go's song."

He stood up and started to dance, moving his hands from side to side and singing "We Got the Beat."

"Bullshit," I said laughing, "I don't have a thing for her. She's just smart and has her shit together."

"Smart is pretty seductive. Think Syd would have given me a shot if I was some dummy?"

I became defensive. "It's not like that. Don't ruin this for me."

"Ruin it, I'm trying to save your ass. How do you think Lexi saw it?"

"Lexi?"

"Yeah, Lexi, that smart, hot-ass girl whose fatal flaw is being with your unwoke ass."

I wanted to laugh, but my head was instantly overwhelmed with the Jessica disaster at Words. I'd thought that was a thing with Lexi and never even considered Jessica could be part of it.

"I would chase that down with her, before it gets out of hand."

I resisted for a moment, but then shot Lexi a text and asked if I could stop by to talk for a minute and received a one-letter reply: *K.*

I got my book bag and thanked Mrs. McDougal for the great dinner. At the door I asked McDougal if he was all right.

"No," he said in a thin, cracking voice, "I'm fucking dying, but I'm going to do some homework listening to Angel Olsen, feel sorry for myself, and get through it."

He raised his hand for a fist bump, but I grabbed it, pulled him close, said, "Thanks," and was off.

At Lexi's I instantly got the vibe that something was indeed wrong. Sitting on her shaky porch steps while I stood over her, she barely looked at me. When I told her about our little Jameson scam and how McDougal was dying because of the Syd thing, all she could muster was a couple of one-word responses.

Getting nowhere with small talk, I gathered my courage and said, "Bullshitting tonight, McDougal pointed out I may have been a little overenthusiastic about Jessica at the wake, and I just want to tell—"

She put up her hand to stop me, finally cracking a smile. "You're so clueless sometimes, Jackson. I'm not threatened by Jessica."

"Oh good, I told McDougal he was wrong."

"Oh, he's not wrong. Helen Keller could see that you were totally crushing on her."

"Wait . . . what?"

"It's okay, Jackson. I get it. She's almost perfect, like in a Michelle Obama kind of way. Pretty, smart, passionate."

"No, but . . ."

"Just forget it. It's fine."

"But . . ."

"Jackson . . ."

"Okay," I said, not feeling like I'd had my say, "so what's with the lack of eye contact and the one-word answers?"

"I'm depressed about James and Syd—and us."

"Us, why us? You just said . . ."

"I know what I said and I feel really close to you, it's just—it's just all too soon. Everything with us is happening too soon. If we were sophomores in college maybe, but we're high schoolers."

"Lex, you're overthinking this. It's fine. We're cool."

"It's not fine. Both of us got all this out-of-control shit around us, ready to take us down. How are we ever going to last?"

"Lex . . ."

"My father came by today, first time in months, and right away there's a big fight."

"That's not us, that's them. We're better than they are."

"Really?" she said, standing up. "I took a swing at him. How much better is that?"

I laughed. "You took a swing at him. Why?"

"You don't want to know."

"Yes I do."

"He's such a clueless asshole. How could my mom let a jerk like that knock her up—

twice?"

"C'mon, why'd you try to hit him?"

"Jackson . . ."

"Tell me."

She sighed, looked at me with a certain deliberateness, and said, "I was up in my room and heard some loud voices. I wasn't sure who it was until I was about halfway down the stairs. When I figured it out, I was just going to avoid it and go back up to my room, but I heard my mom crying so I went into the kitchen, and that asshole looked at me and said, 'And you, going out with some black kid.' I was like, fuck this, and took a wild swing at him."

Smiling, I said, "You little badass. What'd he do?"

"He threw up his hands and said something like, 'I'm outta here,' and left. I just missed busting his skull open."

She was all angry and fiery. I liked her like this and stood there smiling at her, feeling lucky to be with her. She seethed for another minute, and when she finally smiled, I pulled her close and we kissed. After separating we just stared at each other. Still not verbally expressing our feelings, we tried to say it with our eyes. When the extended bit of blissful gazing came to a conclusion, half joking, I said, "You defended my honor."

She turned fiery again and said, "Screw that asshole."

Feeling playful, I said, "C'mon, show me that punch," and we danced around throwing fake punches at each other, discussing new strategies for knocking out, or at least immobilizing, the assholes that were our fathers. She was so pretty and funny, saying, "*pow pow pow*," pretending to pummel me with a barrage of punches.

When that played out, I pulled her close again and kissed her goodbye, then half stated, half asked, "We're good . . . right?"

"Yes," she said with the cutest embarrassed face. "We're good."

Walking home, I shot McDougal a text telling him I smoothed out all the Lexi stuff and asked him how he was doing. He sent back a bunch of sad/angry emoji faces. McDougal hated emojis, which I supposed meant his shit was beyond words at the moment. I sent back a lame *it'll get better* text.

At school the next day on my way to gym class, I saw Syd in the basement hallway. She saw me too and immediately turned around and went the other way. Tap-dancing through hordes of people, I caught up with her just as she was going up the stairs to the first floor.

"Syd, wait."

She turned around and I could see a certain amount of dread in her face, which made me feel awful. "Can we talk? Whaddya have this period?"

"Study hall ."

"C'mon," I said, and I led her by the elbow toward the exit at the bottom of the stairs. The security guard normally there was engaged in some drama in the hallway.

She hesitated at the door and said, "You're not going to yell at me about James, are you? 'Cause I feel bad enough."

"No. I just want to talk."

Outside we were met by bright sunshine and a breeze ripe with the first hints of fall. We quickly crossed the Avenue and headed down a side street struggling to remain viable with a mix of crappy, crumbling houses and houses trying not to be crappy.

Once on the side street we slowed down, and after walking a bit, Syd cautiously asked, "So, you don't hate me?"

"No, I don't hate you."

"I thought for sure you were going to blow me up."

"Maybe before, but not now. I get how hard it was for you to be with him."

"What does that mean?"

"Just that you get a ton of attention and you seem to have a type

159

that isn't McDougal."

"I thought you weren't going to be mean, Jackson."

"I'm not being mean and I'm not judging you. I'm just saying I understand there were things about both of you that were going to make it hard to be together."

"He's like a million times smarter than me. And you too. Even Lexi. When did Lexi get so smart?"

"You're plenty smart, Syd. It's just you're stuck in a bad situation at home."

"No, I hardly ever know what you guys are talking about or read any of those books you talk about, and Jackson . . . I like the Chili Peppers and U2."

"You little philistine. I know I said I wouldn't judge you, but this is beyond bad."

"See, right there," she said with a big smile. "Did you just call me a whore?"

"Whore, no. I called you something far worse—I called you common. Philistine is a bible word for common."

"Yeah, that is bad . . ."

"I'm kidding. You're anything but common."

When we stopped laughing, Syd asked, "Why are you being nice to me? He's like your best friend."

"I can be nice to you and still be best friends with him. All the bullshit that comes with my old man, the hate and anger, it's a lot to carry around. I just don't want to hate . . . anyone."

"Again, right there, you're so smart."

"Not smart. Seeing my grandmother wither away and die . . . I don't know, maybe now I see the world in a bigger way."

She let that sink in for a minute as we plodded along, and then said, "That's some deep shit, Jackson. Maybe U2 could dress it all up and use it in a song."

"Ha. Yeah, that would be great."

She smiled and then asked, "So how's he doing?"

"He's getting through it."

"I never wanted . . ." Her voice trailed off. Then, quietly, she added, "It's better this way, before things got too far."

We had gone around the short block and still had some time to kill before our next class. Standing on the corner, Syd lit a cigarette and after a few pulls handed it to me. "You smoke now?"

"Nah, someone just gave these to me."

I took a hit and immediately started coughing. "Oh my god, that's terrible."

Syd laughed and took the cigarette back. "Like this." She demonstrated, taking a smaller hit.

"Ah." I did it without coughing, but it was still terrible. Just then a kid came out of school, and I yelled for him to hold the door. We threw away the smoke, ran across the street, and ambled into the building. There was still some time before our next class, so we made our way to the basement restrooms with only a sideways glance from a security guard walking the halls. Before we separated, Syd leaned in and hugged me. "Thank you for understanding. Will you tell James . . ." and her voice faded away. But I got it.

"I'll tell him."

"Thank you. Take care, Jackson."

"Yeah, you too, Syd. See ya around."

School policy dictated any unmuted phone would be taken away for the day, and as I settled into a stall, waiting on the bell for class to change, I found a bunch of urgent texts from Lexi saying she needed to talk right away. I replied saying we could talk at lunch after next period. I couldn't imagine what it could be since we were pretty good right now, but there was a real sense of panic in the texts.

The bell rang as I was washing my hands, and rockhead McManus and a couple of his rockhead friends came into the restroom and were like, "There he is, Jackson 'the cuck' Wolf." They laughed and punched each other in the arm. "How's it feel to be a cuck, Wolf?" one of the moron friends said.

I didn't really know what they were talking about and just flipped them off, but I had a feeling it was related to Lexi's texts and was pretty distracted all through World History before lunch.

At lunch both Lexi and McDougal were waiting for me. Before getting anything to eat, she made me sit down. I protested, saying that I was starving and whatever it was could wait while I got the ham-and-cheese melt and sweet potato fries, but Lexi was insistent. Finally, McDougal said, "Gimme your IDs. Ida's at the checkout today—she loves me. I'll get our lunches."

We handed him our IDs, and after raising his eyebrows in a knowing way, he made his way up to the lunch line.

Surrounded by lunchroom commotion, I took a seat across from Lexi, and she wrapped her long, graceful fingers around my hands. A look of concern bordering on panic engulfed her face. Sometimes deep in those pale-blue eyes you could see her wounds, the places where she had been marked by past blows. In those moments she looked so beautifully sad, like a flower taking precarious breaths while lying in the gutter, but this was different. She was scared.

"Jackson," she said, looking me in the eye, "Mr. Jubulis, the AP

Bio teacher, is making me be lab partners with Ted Groman."

"Isn't that your old boyfriend—the Big Star dude with the afro?"

"Yes, the Big Star dude," she said, becoming annoyed. "He's also the person who crushed my heart for half a year."

"Can't you just change partners? You know, tell Jubulis there's extenuating circumstances."

"I did, and Mr. Jubulis asked if anything inappropriate was said or if I felt threatened. I said no but told him there was a history and I feel uncomfortable being Groman's partner. He gave me some shit about not giving my adolescent feelings so much power and since this was a college-level course, we needed to learn not only how to survive challenging situations, but also how to thrive in them."

"Can you drop it?"

"No, I need this class. It's like free college credits."

"What about Groman?"

"He asked too and got the same story about thriving and surviving."

McDougal was back with our food, having shoved everything onto a single tray. As he set the tray down and got situated, I said, "Oh, that's why McManus called me a cuck. No way he's in your AP Bio?"

"No, but he was walking by and stopped when I was arguing with Mr. J. in the hall after class."

Then I said, "Well, it's only two periods a week and I'm not worried about you and Groman." And as I spoke, McDougal, who was sitting next to Lexi, was shaking his head for me to stop, but it was too late.

"Jackson, this isn't about you and what you're worried about, you asshole."

"No, I know. I'm just saying, don't worry about me while you work this out. I'm trying to be supportive."

"Sounds to me like you didn't hear a thing I said and how upset this makes me."

"No, I did, I'm sorry. It's just . . ."

But it was too late. She had gathered her things, got up, and left without eating.

After pointing out how right she was to get mad and that I was a dumbass, McDougal helped me come up with some easy ways for her to stop being partners with Groman. She could tell one of the assistant principals or other school administrators how uncomfortable this pairing was for her, or maybe one of their parents could call the school and complain. It probably wouldn't be that hard at all to get out of it.

"Am I missing something? This seems like an easy fix," I said.

"Yeah, I think all it would take is a phone call or a conversation with an administrator to change it. But she was upset and not seeing it yet, and then you made it about yourself."

"Yeah, don't remind me. Shit!"

"Do you see her again today?"

"Yeah, period after next, we have English together."

"She's going to be starving. It'd be a good idea to get her something."

So I got her a bag of chips and a pack of cookies. Later, in English, when I gave her the snacks, she thanked me and gave me a fleeting smile, but that was it.

It had been a few turbulent days with Syd, Lexi, and McDougal. Though most of it was unpleasant, it felt necessary and instructive and fit nicely with what I told Syd about seeing the world in a bigger way. But this seeing was mostly a reactive, past-tense type of thing that led to me screwing things up. I needed to get my shit together at the front end to avoid all this unpleasant fallout. Try again tomorrow.

CHAPTER 14

SOMETIMES YOU CAN'T see things right in front of you. This lack of vision makes it hard to respond to events in your life in a competent way or to understand the consequences of your actions. And for all my big talk about getting ahead of situations and being proactive, it turned out to be more of a fleeting intention rather than something I was able to put into practice.

That said, Lexi took the unusual move of sticking it out with Groman, refusing to find another way *not* to be his lab partner. She was going to show Mr. Jubulis that she could not only survive, but indeed thrive in any situation you threw at her. It was really uncomfortable at first, but she found a way to get through it and was really proud of herself. I was proud and happy for her too and wasn't threatened by this Groman kid at all. At first, I even felt an affinity for him through Big Star, but I was hearing the "cuck" talk, which grew increasingly annoying. Every time McManus and his crew saw me, they would make this "cucking" sound, which simulated the sound of a quacking duck. It became a game of trying to get me to react, but I was mostly able to ignore it. The problem was Lexi became a little too chummy with Groman.

She started walking in the halls with him after class, and not only did the McManus shit intensify, but I also got looks from others and I heard the whispers behind my back.

"We're only walking to class. Do you not trust me?" she asked.

"Of course I trust you, but the cucking shit is starting to come at me from all directions."

"Can't you just ignore it?"

"I have been ignoring it, but you walking the halls with him doesn't help."

"We're just walking . . ."

"Really, Lexi?" I said, becoming frustrated. "You don't get how walking the halls with your ex-boyfriend blows back on me?"

"Okay . . . okay," she said, rolling her eyes.

"What's with the eye roll?"

"Jackson . . ."

"Don't 'Jackson' me. This is bullshit." And I stormed off.

Working out after school in McDougal's garage, I was still pissed and tried to excise my anger away by doing a million push-ups and pull-ups. Still depressed about Syd, McDougal bombed out quickly and waited for me to tell him what was up while he sat, fidgeting with his phone, sipping Gatorade. When that didn't quite work, a hilarious song by Yo La Tengo called "Mr. Tough" came into the mix and McDougal got up and mimicked the tune, which was about rivals settling their differences on the dance floor. The little hobbit was so funny dancing to the playful melody, I couldn't help but join in. His mom pulled up right in the middle of our little dance off and with a smile said, "I don't even want to know," as she made her way through the garage.

When the tune ended, I explained my pissy mood. "She was walking the halls with Groman after class both today and Monday, and the cucking shit is starting to get out of hand."

"Yeah, I've been hearing people say stuff too."

"She got a bit of an attitude when I explained it."

"Ah, hence the Navy Seal routine here."

"Am I wrong?"

"No, that's bullshit on her part, one hundred percent. And trust me, if you were wrong, I'd let you know. It's one of the few joys I have these days."

I laughed appreciatively and said, "Thanks." Preoccupied with Groman, I hadn't told McDougal yet about talking with Syd. "Hey, so I ducked out of gym the other day and talked to Syd."

"And?"

"Sorry, dude," I said, trying to deliver the blow as gently as possible.

His shoulders sort of folded in and he looked away. "What'd she say?"

"Said you were a great guy and she feels awful."

"What else?"

"You're too smart for her."

"Ah, bullshit. That's her stuff at home."

"Was my point too, and she said she never knew what we were talking about, that she couldn't keep up."

"You were nice to her?"

"Yes, sir . . . Except for the part where I busted her chops about liking the Chili Peppers and U2."

"If she could get past her present . . . she'd see," he said cryptical-ly.

"What's that mean?"

"C'mon, Jackson, who'd be better for her than me?"

"No one, but she's not there."

"She will be. I'll wait it out."

"Dude."

"What?" he said with an edge.

As gently as I could, I said, "She's not there. Time to turn the page."

"Fuck off, Jackson."

"There's plenty of other girls."

"Fuck y—" And before he could get it out, he dropped his head and brought his hands up to his face.

I pulled him in and said, "There's lots of girls. I see them looking at you."

"Who?" he said with just a hint of a quiver in his voice.

"That little girl I see doing my Pennysaver route . . . Olivia . . . Olivia O'Malley. She even asked me one day if I was friends with you."

"Olivia O'Malley has been eyeballing me since sixth grade. And you're only bringing her up 'cause she's small."

She was small like him, but that's not why. "Bullshit," I said. "That girl is really cute and she takes the same brainy classes as you."

"Yeah, but . . ."

"Yeah, but what? Are you too good or something?"

"No, she's just . . . I don't know . . . ancient history."

"Why? She's really cute. Time to check her out."

"Don't think so. I'm past her. I might throw some lines at Jasmine Hunter . . . Go big or go home, right?"

"Yeah, you and Jasmine." I laughed 'cause Jasmine was the six-foot-three star basketball player at our school. "You guys would be the dopest couple ever."

"I was walking behind her in the hall the other day and she

dropped her pen. I grabbed it and called to her, and when she turned around, her lady pecs were right in my eyes," he said with a smile.

"Did she catch you, 'cause I know your pervy ass couldn't turn away."

"Not true, I was totally smooth. I gave her pen back and she smiled at me and said thanks."

"And . . ."

"And . . . what? I smiled back and said, 'You're welcome.'"

"And?"

"And . . . what?"

"C'mon . . . Cut it out. What was the disgusting thing that went through your head next?"

"Whaddya mean disgusting? It's not disgusting to think about how those pecs could potentially blind a guy like me. That's not disgusting—that's my survival instincts kicking in."

"You're such an asshole."

"Thank you."

"But if you really like her, I see her at the library sometimes and could talk to her for you."

"She's pretty smoking. What's she doing at the library?"

"Probably the same thing everyone does at the library—reading—but I've never talked to her."

"Think she's avoiding shit at home like you?"

"How the hell do I know?"

"Well . . ."

"Ah, I get you, 'cause we're both black."

"Yeah, that's it, 'cause you're black. No, you dummy, 'cause you're both at the fucking library reading when you should be home bullying people online."

It was good to hear him joke like this. With each passing day the grip on his relationship with Syd was loosening bit by bit, despite the occasional setback.

And while his reality was slowly getting better, mine was getting worse. I was standing with Lexi at her locker a few days later and Groman came up and started talking to her with me right there. To be fair, it was about some lab bullshit he needed from her, but I didn't care and was like, "Are you crazy? Get the out of here."

"Jackson," Lexi said.

"Don't 'Jackson' me, Lexi. Beat it."

But he just stood there with this dumb look on his face, and Lexi, shuffling through her folder, said, "He just needs my data."

"I don't care what he needs," I said, looking at Lexi. Then I turned to Groman and said, "It's your choice, dude. You can just leave or you can leave with a broken fucking face, but one thing is for sure—you're leaving."

He chose to leave with his face intact, but after finding the paper, Lexi took off after him and as she was leaving said, "What is wrong with you?"

And from there it only got worse. I got a text from her one day the next week before lunch saying she had to sit with Groman at lunch to finish up some work. We had been talking about it here and there, but when this lunch bullshit happened, I communicated my displeasure forcefully as we walked down the Avenue after school.

"How hard is this class that you always have to get together with him?"

"You're being dramatic. It was one time at lunch, and it was because I forgot to do something. And it's AP Bio—it's really hard."

"You're taking other AP classes and you're not getting together with anyone from those classes."

"Jackson, you're in my AP English and we talk all the time about it. Remember the metaphor conversation about the Mississippi?"

We did have a long conversation about how each new situation presented in Huck Finn, as he rolled down the Mississippi, was a kind of galaxy unto itself, but still. "Why can't you do this shit at the library?"

"The library?"

"Yeah, it's that quiet place at the end of my street."

"Jackson, you're making more of this than you need to."

"Why are you fighting me on this? Don't you get the bullshit I have to put up with? How people look at me?"

"Jackson."

"No, don't 'Jackson' me. If you don't get it, do it because I'm asking you, just like you asked me not to use the *love* word, as silly as that is."

"It's not silly . . ." But she stopped there and for a moment considered what I had said. Then the fierceness that had come onto her face dripped away, and she said, "Okay, I get it. I'm sorry. I'll do better." And she sealed the promise by leaning in with a beautiful Lexi kiss.

Even though the cucking and whispers continued, over the next few weeks Lexi did live up to her part of the deal and limited her contact with him to the Bio lab. She did say that Groman had made overtures about getting back together, but she was so adamant about it never happening I didn't feel the least bit threatened. I complimented her on how impressive it was she could keep all this in check and how she set such a good example for me to follow.

We were sitting on her steps at the time, and she guided me up to my feet and wrapped her arms around me. She pulled herself tight against my body and then kissed me and said, "I love you, Jackson."

My head nearly exploded. I kissed her again and said, "You are so unbelievable. I love you too."

Then that fabulous turning point, that upping of our game, turned to shit a few days later when I missed a text from her and found them sitting together at lunch. I sat down in a huff, and McDougal tried to cool my jets by reminding me how everything had been really good lately. He also said I maybe should concede the point on Groman, accept they were going to be spending time together, become friends with him, even.

But as Lexi was putting some folders in her handbag, from across the room Groman smiled and waved at me in this snarky kind of way, and I lost my shit. Against McDougal's objections, I got up and walked past eight or ten tables, gaining momentum as I moved. Lexi was just standing up, gathering her things to leave, and said, "Jackson."

But I ignored her and to Groman said, "Who the fuck you waving at, asshole?" I knocked his and the next kid's over's lunch trays to the floor. He stood up like he was going to do something, while Lexi tried to push me away and yelled, "Jackson!" with McDougal also chiming in.

But I was undeterred and said, "C'mon, fucker, let's do this," and I started for him across the table, but was thwarted from behind by Mr. Franklin and another security guard before I could get at him.

Locking up my arms, they proceeded to drag me from the cafeteria while I yelled dumb threats at Groman amid a smattering of cucking sounds. By the time the guards had me in the hallway outside the cafeteria, I was out of breath and already starting to regret my actions.

Sitting in detention trying to read my Junot Díaz book, I had this ominous feeling and couldn't concentrate. I kept thinking about the path of least resistance McDougal had suggested, which meant becoming friends with Groman. Sitting there, I realized it was the obvious thing to do all along, and I was embarrassed that I'd missed it. Why was I fighting this? Lexi not only was with me, but she loved me, and I loved her. It was just so obvious. All the shit that came with fighting it, like the cucking, would go away once I stopped allowing it to piss me off. It was so simple and I felt so dumb for not seeing it.

But it was too late. When my phone was returned to me after school, I saw Lexi's text from before lunch saying she had to spend five minutes with Groman and then would be over to sit with McDougal and me. She signed the text, which she hardly ever did, with, *Love, your girl*. She added *xoxoxoxo*, along with some heart emojis. This was bad. I sent her a text saying what a dumbass I was and how I was so, so sorry for causing that scene in the cafeteria. To which I received total silence. I walked/ran to her house, but she wasn't there. I went to The Spot, sent several more texts to no avail, and then headed for home.

When I got there, Lexi was sitting on our badly worn porch steps. I could tell she had been crying. I sat down next to her and after a muffled greeting launched into the apology I had been texting her.

She stood up, shook her head, and with tears in her eyes said, "Jackson, we can't be together anymore."

"No, I'm sorry. Sitting in detention today I finally got it," I said, standing up. "I finally realized that fighting the Groman thing was stupid, that I should make friends with him. Really."

"I want things, Jackson. Things that are hard for people like us to get, and I can't be dragged down by this anymore."

"You're right. I'm sorry. I get it now. I know I was letting the taunting get to me. I gave it power, but I'm past that now. No more drama."

But she just stood there shaking her head. "I came a long way with you, Jackson. You helped me see that I could be more, and I'll always be grateful to you for that, but I just can't . . ."

"Lex, it doesn't have to be like this."

With tears pouring from her eyes, she leaned in and kissed me on the cheek. "Goodbye, Jackson." And then she turned and scurried away, half walking, half running.

Stunned, I sat down on the steps and just flatlined for I don't know how long. When the old man pulled the Ranger into the driveway, I snapped back to reality. It was Thursday, so he didn't have much money and his buzz was of the moderate sort.

"What the fuck you doing just sitting there?"

"I don't feel good. I'm going to bed."

I went upstairs, and my phone dinged. It was one of several texts from McDougal that I'd missed in my dazed state on the steps. With a certain urgency he asked where I was and what happened. There was also a text from Lexi sent shortly after she left here, saying she was blocking my number, which was like a knife twisting in my side. This was really happening.

With tears in my eyes, I sent a short text to McDougal telling him Lexi dumped me and that I was going to bed and would talk to him in the morning. He hit me back right away with a *K* and a sad-face emoji with a tear.

I took off my shoes and pants, curled up in a little ball under my ratty blanket and began to weep softly. The tears embarrassed me and for a while I tried to fight them, but her text telling me she had blocked my number was so hopeless and final that I just surrendered and cried till I drifted off.

The old man was already gone for work when I woke up in the morning feeling more exhausted than when I went to bed. Right away I knew that I didn't have the strength or courage to face any school bullshit today and sent McDougal a text telling him I was staying home. He hit me back saying he had his first big test of the year in Algebra 3 second period and would skip out after that and come to the house.

He showed up with a couple of Tim Horton double doubles and some donuts about midmorning. Feeling like a million pound weight was sitting on my shoulders, I made space for the Timmy Ho's on the coffee table by taking some empty beer cans and ashtrays into the kitchen. When I came back McDougal asked, "So, how ya doing?"

I couldn't answer because if I did, I was going to start bawling. Fighting it, I stared at the floor, but it was useless and tears started to fall from my eyes. Embarrassed, I continued to stare at the floor, but then I heard a muffled sort of groan from McDougal. I looked at him and his eyes were wet. He came over, put his head on my chest, and hugged me. I not only hugged him back, I clung to him, holding on for dear life. We stood like that till our wells ran dry and when McDougal pulled away, wiping his eyes, he said, "You get dumped by one girl and you yammer on like the worst kind of drama queen."

I laughed, spraying tears and snot through the room. "Ha, kiss my ass, you little snowflake."

We sat down and he handed me a few napkins and my coffee. This was the first time McDougal had been in my house, and as I got my shit together, he looked around at the peeling wallpaper, the torn furniture, the threadbare rug, and the brake pads and rotors on the floor, and deadpanned, "So, this is nice," and we both cracked up again.

We hit our coffees and I took a bite of a glazed old fashion that burned my teeth. Still a few weeks before the election, when I turned on the TV, Trump was yelling about Crooked Hillary and what a shithole the country was and how he was going to make it great again. Ughhh.

We found a morning block of *Bob's Burgers* on the Cartoon Network and settled in watching it. Other than a few laughs at the show, we didn't say much to each other, and I only got through about half of my coffee and one more bite of a donut. After two or three episodes, during one of the commercials McDougal hit the mute button on the remote and said, "Next time, both of us need to think what it'll be like without them. Plan ahead for when they're gone. It'll make it hurt less when they dump us."

He hit the sound again and despite feeling a little hopeless, I thought, *Of course.* That would be a purposeful act of self-preservation and not just some goddamn fleeting intention. It was getting ahead of a situation and being proactive in your life.

CHAPTER 15

A S I RODE the waves of this doomed relationship in the weeks following Lexi dumping me, my moods were in a constant state of flux. Sometimes it was inconceivable that she was gone, and sometimes I got very pissed she dumped me just when I had the Groman thing figured out. Lexi was having a hard time too, keeping mostly to herself in the halls and sitting alone or with Syd at lunch. As sad as it sounds, it was a big relief she was having a hard time. Had she moved on like I never meant anything to her, that maybe would have been worse than just being dumped. I know it was petty and vindictive, but in a weird way it helped that she was messed up too.

Syd, for her part, seemed to have completely left McDougal in the dust, eagerly consuming the endless attention that came at her from all directions. Some of this attention from the guys stopping by their lunch table flowed naturally to Lexi, but she wasn't having it. She either shut them down or got up and left. This gave me a ray of hope that somehow there was still a chance for us, especially when after several agonizing weeks of not even making eye contact, we nodded at each other in English class. But when I said, "Hello," after a few days of nodding, she shut me down too and I briefly tumbled back into a depressive state.

I don't know what it was or what snapped, but sitting in English one day, still depressed, wishing she would look my way again, I realized I was ceding all my power to this stupid breakup. All my energy was going to something that was dead, and like the Groman thing, which eventually became so obvious, just like that, I finally accepted it was over with Lexi.

Around that time I saw Reese Witherspoon on a magazine cover at the library, and next to her big toothy picture was a caption: "No Regrets." I hate that fucking cowboy "no regrets" shit, especially with the rise of Trump. I mean, really Reese, you never messed something up, hurt someone, were selfish and stupid and wished you pursued a different course of action? It's so dumb and egotistical and why America sucks. I regret loads of shit, especially how I blew everything up with Lexi. We had so much fun, she was so beautiful, and we grew so much together, and my stupid pride brought it all down.

More than a month removed, fully understanding we were done, I looked at Lexi one day in English and rather than longing for her, I was filled with admiration. In spite of the odds against a person like her, she knew what she wanted and was going for it, fueled by nothing more than grit and determination. I'll never forget how she transformed right before my eyes from this little lost girl into this rugged, tenacious person. And though it was too soon, I hoped to thank her one day for what she said about coming a long way with me and how I showed her she could be more. All of that certainly wasn't me, but I'll never forget the grace she showed me in our darkest moment or that she was the first girl, or really, the first person, whom I was incalculably, unabashedly in love with and who was in love with me.

I also wouldn't forget how she crushed me. It might be a little cynical, but I'm not going into another relationship anytime soon without an exit strategy, without a safety net. There was pain when my mom and my grandmother left, and the old man had been known to inflict some serious blows too, but nothing ever hurt as much as being dumped by Lexi. The desolation and hopelessness were beyond words. So, going forward, as an act of self-preservation, I was determined to treat any and all relationships as impermanent. Like McDougal said, plan for when they're gone, so when they dump us, it won't hurt so bad.

But it wasn't only relationships with girls that were impermanent. Everything more or less was transitory, and when one storm passed, the only thing you could be sure of was there would be more storms, storms that you couldn't plan for or escape, storms that just poured down from the sky, where the only thing you could do was take cover.

In the weeks leading up to the election, the old man was crazed. Depending on the Fox News segment, he was either yelling, "Fuck Crooked Hillary," at the TV or brooding about the conspiracy Trump was pushing that the presidency was going to be stolen from him. As we replaced some sections of fencing for our neighbor Mrs. Hagan the Saturday before the election, all he could talk about was building the wall on Mexico's dime, repealing and replacing Obamacare with something great, suspending immigration from terrorist countries, and "winning," so much "winning" we were going to get sick of it. It was nauseating, to the point where I finally told him about Lexi dumping me.

"Is that why you've been such a fucking mope?"

"A mope?"

"Yeah, besides sleeping about twenty hours a day, you've been moping around here like a man-baby."

"I haven't been sleeping that much."

He rolled his eyes in disbelief and said, "How'd you fuck it up?"

"What makes you think I fucked it up?"

"If you didn't, you wouldn't be such a mope."

"Good point," I said, smiling. "She was in a class with an old boyfriend, and the dude sort of taunted me. I made a big scene at lunch."

"Did you kick his ass?" he asked with a laugh.

"Didn't get that far."

"What was her name . . . Alexa?"

"Yeah, Lexi."

"Pretty girl. Too good for your sorry ass." He smiled.

And except for a nod or two and a couple of grunts, that was pretty much the last conversation we ever had.

I got home from McDougal's and the library just past 9 p.m. on election night, and there were empty beer cans all over the living room along with a fifth of Black Velvet that was a third of the way gone. I grabbed some empties as I walked into the kitchen and asked, "How's it going?"

"It's going great. The people are taking back America tonight. MAGA . . . MAGA . . . MAGA."

I went upstairs and read a bit of *Sound and Fury* and fell asleep. I was occasionally awoken by shouts of "OHIO" and "FLORI-DA" as Trump won those states. Then finally, at 3 a.m. when they called it for Trump, the old man was out in the street, dancing around, screaming: "MAGA . . . MAGA . . . MAGA . . . DONALD TRUMP . . . TRUMP . . . TRUMP . . . TRUMP."

I got up, put on a hoodie, and went outside to try and get him before the cops showed up. Mrs. Hagan was already out there at the end of her driveway, yelling at him to "shut up." And then, just as I was coming down the front steps, he tripped on a hole in the pavement and went face-first to the ground, hitting his forehead on the curb with a giant *thud*. Never did a sound cut through the air with more grimness and finality. Mrs. Hagan was over to his listless body first and in a dire tone said, "Oh, Jackson, this is bad. Call an ambulance."

The cops had probably been on the way because of his yelling, and two squad cars were there when I came flying back out of the house after calling 911. Before I could get to the old man, the cop standing with Mrs. Hagan, Officer Kennedy, stopped me and walked me a few houses down the street and very calmly asked me about the events of the night. Soon, a third and a fourth cop car along with the ambulance showed up. There was a lot of activity, a perimeter was secured, and one of the paramedics was yelling, "AIS6," but from the inert way he was lying there I knew it was all for nothing.

As Officer Kennedy continued to engage me and direct my eyes away from the old man's spent body in the street, he turned down the radio that was clipped to a strap at his shoulder where the other officers were talking about a "10-55." Officer Kennedy then informed me we would be going to the station house and put me in the car and asked Mrs. Hagan, who was still standing close by, to lock up the house. Even though Officer Kennedy kept telling me, "Eyes up front," I looked back as we pulled away, and through a small hole in the gathering crowd standing around the perimeter, I saw a paramedic unfurl a sheet and begin to lower it. I didn't actually see it cover the old man's body, but after watching my share of *Law & Order* episodes with my grandmother, I had no trouble envisioning the image.

Though my mind raced in a million different directions, once we were riding down my street, I morbidly couldn't resist doing a Google search on AIS6—abbreviated injury scale, 6 was maximum severity. A 10-55 was a coroner's case.

Moving down the Avenue with this ominous information in my head, I became detached from what was going on, like I was watching a dumb *Law & Order* episode and this wasn't really happening to me. But when Officer Kennedy began to talk, asking if there was other family I could contact, it all became very real, because there really wasn't any other family and suddenly, in a panic, I felt totally alone. In spite of everything, the one reliable thing about the old man was he was always present. Even when he was on the periphery or when he was being a violent, drunk asshole, he was at least present. And now that he was gone, I was overwhelmed by my aloneness.

The only person I thought to call was McDougal, which Officer Kennedy said was fine, but unless I came up with some legitimate family, they were going to have to refer me to Child Protective Services. Then I remembered the old man had a cousin, Teddy. When I told Officer Kennedy, he was like, "Teddy Wolf, oh yeah, we know him."

I had to dial McDougal a couple of times before he picked up, but once I got through to him, he and his mom were at the station in no time. Through the glass doors of the waiting room where I was sitting, I saw them come in and talk to the officer at the front desk. McDougal entered the room and gave me a hug and said, "Uh . . . sorry 'bout your dad," while his mom got the rundown from Officer Kennedy outside the waiting room. When his mom was done, she came in and hugged me too. I felt very safe with them there, and as she continued to hug me, I had to fight back the tears welling in my eyes.

Though the police put in calls to the old man's cousin, Teddy, several hours passed without any response. Given that I was a minor, for legal reasons, there could be no statement regarding my old man's status until a next of kin was present. While we waited we looked through the glass doors at what was going down at the front desk, fidgeted with our phones, and occasionally gave each other stiff smiles, but there wasn't much talking. I was taking in images, reading posts, looking at bike tricks on YouTube, but nothing was really registering. Prior to Officer Kennedy's shift ending at 7 a.m., McDougal's mom spoke with him again and then he approached me, shook my hand firmly, and told me to "hang tough." Giving a nod to McDougal's mom, he said, "You're in good hands."

Once he was gone, McDougal's mom, staring straight ahead, said in a matter-of-fact tone, "Jackson, when this is all over, would you like to come and stay with James and me on a permanent basis?"

Sitting there, trying to metabolize what she said, I already felt like I was fading out of one life into another, whether I liked it or not. When I didn't answer, she turned to me, took my hands, and with a reassuring smile said, "It'll be nice to have you in the family. You'll have to bunk with James when my parents come up from Florida in the summer, but otherwise you can have their room. It'll be nice for all of us. Would you like that?"

Just then an officer brought the old man's cousin, Teddy, into the room, saving me from trying to come up with an answer. I almost laughed out loud. He was the same disheveled, unshaven, reeking-of-last-night's-booze guy as the old man, but in a forest-green work uniform with an oval name tag above his shirt pocket that said *Teddy*.

Finally, with next of kin present, I was informed of the passing of my old man and was released to Teddy after he signed some papers.

Outside, Teddy looked at me and said, "Sorry about Mickey," and then to McDougal's mom, "Call me if you need anything." With that he got into a beat-up Subaru and was off.

We stopped at a Greek diner called the Apollo for breakfast, and McDougal's mom informed us that to avoid me being placed with Child Protective Services, she'd worked out a deal with Officer Kennedy and Teddy to take me home. In the coming days, with the cooperation of Teddy, we were going to have to meet with social workers to begin the adoption process. Still numb and overwhelmed from last night's turn of events, I struggled to process everything she was telling me. I nodded without really understanding what she was saying. When we got to McDougal's, I lay down in what I guessed was my new bed and passed out until seven o'clock that night.

When I got up, sitting in the kitchen with McDougal's mom were my grandmother's old friends Barb and Patty. After extending their condolences, they explained how they had made a pact with my grandmother before she was ill to look out for the old man, and then they cautiously started to ask questions about what I wanted for a wake and funeral. I was still pretty foggy and heard what they were saying but had zero ability to respond. I looked at McDougal's mom, who understood my confusion, and she cut them off and said she had a plate for me and I should go wash up.

She called to McDougal, who led me back to his room. On the way he said, "They've been here for an hour asking a million questions. How you doing, man?"

"I'm not sure. Everything seems so unreal and shit's happening so fast, I can't really comprehend it."

"And fucking Trump is the president."

"Holy shit, that's right. Trump is the president."

After they were gone, I ate a big chicken breast, some mashed potatoes, and all the asparagus McDougal's mom had made, while McDougal flew through his Algebra equations next to me. His mom moved with grace as she did little tasks around the kitchen, occasionally smiling at me in a reassuring way. Though everything was still pretty surreal, the thing that sort of grounded me and was most real was the PBS NewsHour in the background doing a deep dive into election results. Though I had zero idea how to process the fact I would never smell the old man's boozy breath again or see those watery, crazed eyes, the NewsHour was a cold reminder that life moves on regardless of who you are or what happens to you.

When I finished eating, it was a little too chilly to hang in the garage, so we went to McDougal's room, where I stretched out on his bed looking at my phone while he sat at his desk working on his laptop. His English teacher, Mr. Kane, had a satire website called Buffalomud.com, and he'd commissioned McDougal to optimize the site's speed and functionality. He dialed up some old-school Joy Division, saying he would go a different way if it was too down, but Ian Curtis's melancholic drawl was a perfect match for my numb head. Laughing, McDougal read a couple of titles from the website: "Local Author Thinks He Might Have a Shot with Uma Thurman,"

"South Buffalo Man Misplaces His Ass," "South Buffalo Man Finds Misplaced Ass." I had seen Mr. Kane's site and liked it, but nothing was landing on me tonight.

I went to bed again an hour or so later after thanking both Mc-Dougal and his mom. I woke up about three in the morning, and my head was a bit clearer. Through the darkness I looked around at my upgraded living conditions and took a deep breath. Uprooted again, I quietly wept, longing for my shithole room and my copy of *The Sound and the Fury*. Lying there after I was all cried out, thinking about my new situation, I found it was impossible to block out the visuals of the old man tripping and hitting his forehead so perfectly on that curb or the paramedic unfurling that sheet to cover his dead body. I smiled thinking how only moments before, drunk off his ass, he was in such a state of elation, enjoying a victory that was so important to him. While denied the secondary triumph of taunting snowflake liberal elites, the fucker still went out on top. That was something. How funny was life that this lowlife prick pulled a rabbit out of his ass and took his exit on such a high?

I tried to hold him in this light, to think of him with compassion, but my thoughts grew dark. Others, like my grandmother, had to go through the suffering and indignity of a slow, painful death, while the old man escaped in an instant. It didn't seem fair that after a lifetime of not being responsible or accountable, he got to exit with one deadly blow. If fate was going to hold anyone accountable and inflict some real pain, you'd think it would be on a perpetually drunk asshole like him. I know in the end we came to a hard-won peace and I was grateful for that, but this just didn't seem fair. I felt bad for having these thoughts while his body had been cold less than twenty-four hours, but not that bad.

The wake itself, as you might imagine, was not a well-attended affair. Some sad fuckers from the neighborhood bars along with guys he worked jobs with paid their respects, extended condolences, and then had beers in the parking lot. A big, imposing guy, thick with booze, said he was the old man's foreman and gave me his last bit of pay, five hundred dollars cash. He told me, "No one could swing a hammer like Mickey Wolf."

It was a nice thing to hear and true. During the roofing jobs this past summer and patch jobs around my grandmother's and the house on Lockwood, one thing was clear: the old man could measure, cut, and secure most anything till it was shored up and impervious to every kind of weather. I needed to hear these things because it was hard, even now, to keep his darkness at bay.

Syd and Lexi came to the wake. Syd was quite comfortable saying hello to McDougal and his mom and hugged me sweetly. She said sorry in a really matter-of-fact way, which I understood and didn't begrudge her one bit. Lexi, on the other hand, was very uncomfortable, whispering a "sorry about your old man" condolence, barely looking me in the eye.

While Syd talked to an equally uncomfortable McDougal and his mom, Lexi went over to the kneeling rail to pay her respects. On the inside ledge of the puffy white lining of the casket there were some framed pictures of the old man and his father and one with my grandmother in their younger days, sporting big smiles. Over Lexi's back, her beautiful sandy hair sitting on her shoulders, you could see the smiling picture of the old man and my grandmother, and suddenly, as if in the frame of another picture, I had a startling revelation. All three of them—my grandmother, Lexi, and the old man—had left me and were gone from my life. This

discovery shook me to my core, and when Lexi was upright again
I could barely thank her as she made her way to the exit, fearing
that I might lose my shit and start bawling. After she and Syd left, I
went to the restroom, took some deep breaths, but remained fixated
on the idea that everyone in my life was leaving me: my mom, my
grandmother, Lexi, and now the old man. As I was explaining this
to McDougal, pins and needles crawled up the back of my neck,
and all at once I understood he would be next. McDougal was going to be the next person to leave me.

Chapter 16

As it turned out, it wasn't McDougal who would be leaving. It was Jessica Lee. Her boyfriend was a hotshot software engineer and she was going with him down to Tampa, Florida, to work for some startup that implemented GPS systems. Even though it wasn't her area of expertise, in the time before she left she was really supportive with the adoption process, putting us in contact with a friend from school who helped us navigate the system.

A short time after the funeral, I met Jessica at Words for coffee, and she was also very helpful disentangling my complex feelings toward the old man and the idea everyone was leaving me. First, she told me about the five stages of grief: denial, anger, bargaining, depression, and acceptance. Aside from the first twenty-four hours or so, where I was pretty numb and couldn't process, part of the denial step, I seemed to have skipped steps two, three, and four, going directly to acceptance. Jessica thought I might have already internalized those steps after years of dealing with my old man's alcoholism and his more violent tendencies. She highly recommended counseling and told me to be on the lookout for extended states of depression or angry, irrational outbursts.

Even though some of the stages didn't seem to apply or were latent, I bought into the five stages of grief. One by one, they all came into play after Lexi dumped me. It was sad that I had more feeling for a relationship that lasted less than a year than for my old man.

"I know you feel that way now and it's completely valid, but with time and perspective that could change," she conjectured.

"Whaddya mean?"

"Just that as you get older and you gain more experience or get new information, you might realize what your father was up against and consider him in a different way."

"Like have a Buddha moment about the old man?"

"Yes, that's possible."

"Wow, that would be something. But I don't see it . . . ever."

"Jackson, your father didn't get to where he was in life because drinking and fighting was fun or healthy. Somewhere along the way he was grievously injured, and this is how he chose to deal with it."

"I remember my grandmother telling my mom, before she left, that he was just like his father."

"And how old was your grandfather when he died?"

"I don't know. His fifties maybe, before I was around."

"So he was a little further along than your father, but in the same general time frame."

"Yeah, I guess."

"I know you're ready to move on, but you still have to go through his things at your old house. Maybe there's a clue or two there that might give you some perspective down the line. Have a conversation with his cousin . . . What's his name?"

"Teddy."

"Yes, Teddy. See if he has any insights."

I guess her telling me to leave myself open to the possibility of some new kind of epiphany made sense, but what stuck with me and gave me great caution was the idea of "moving on." I wasn't ready, and in all honesty, I was scared moving on would just cause me to lose McDougal and his mom.

"Why can't I just do what I've been doing? Go to McDougal's after school, scam a dinner, then go to the library and home. The only thing different is the old man won't be there screaming about goddamn liberal snowflakes."

"Jackson," she said, frowning.

"Okay, okay . . . but I'm like five for five."

"Five for five?"

"Yeah, everyone I care about—one, my mom; two, my grand-mother; three, Lexi; four, the old man; five, you—leaves."

She smiled, put a hand on my forearm, and said, "Thank you, but I'm not really leaving. I'm a direct flight away, and there's a million different ways to connect."

"Okay," I said with a nod, not really believing her.

"Now let's go through this. Your mom, abusive relationship without any support, right?"

"My grandmother."

"I'm sure your grandmother was great, but that's not the same as her own mom or sisters or brothers."

"Yes, point taken."

"Are you interested in seeing your mom again?"

"Yeah, sure."

"Okay, maybe there's some clue to where she is in your father's stuff. I'll help you with that. But let's not get sidetracked by that now. Next, your grandmother. She was ill and severely disabled. Right?"

"Right."

"Lexi, a high school romance. I'm not dismissing it or trying to invalidate any feelings you had or still have for her. Lord knows how I was crushed junior year when Jimmy Velasquez dumped me. High school is synonymous with change. You had other girlfriends before Lexi, right?"

"Yes."

"And even though Lexi was more serious, you moved on from them."

"Yeah, I guess."

"And your father. It probably happened sooner than it should have, but like his father, he was on a really self-destructive path. Right?"

"Right."

"And me. We already established I'm not really going away. Do you see what I'm getting at here, Jackson?"

"Um . . . No, not really."

"In each case, with the exception of Lexi, you've had zero control over any of these things you think are happening to you. And we can explain what happened with Lexi."

I sat for a moment with this and couldn't find a flaw in what she was saying, and then that line from Nirvana came into my head. "Just because you're paranoid doesn't mean they're not after you."

"Didn't know you were a *Catch-22* fan."

"Nirvana."

"Cobain stole it from Joseph Heller."

"Really? How very Coldplay of him."

"Let's not get sidetracked here. I understand you're focusing on this pattern where everyone is leaving you. Let's think about it for a moment again: your mom escaped an abusive relationship, your grandmother had a catastrophic illness, your father had a freak accident, a girlfriend moved on, and a friend is seeking a new opportunity. Except for your mom, it all fell on you in a short time frame, like an avalanche, but none of it is like a mythical curse. It can all be easily explained. Also, by your logic, not moving on reinforces the cycle of loss."

Although I couldn't argue her points, I didn't feel them, but of course just like she said, doing a deeper dive into life brought new revelations, leading me to consider the old man in a different light. Turned out there was more family besides Teddy, but they all had shunned him and my grandmother when he insisted on marrying my mom—which softened how I saw him.

And then I found pictures of him and my mom in the night table next to the bed where he slept with her. While the old man wasn't exactly smiling in any of the hazy pictures, he didn't look unhappy next to my beautiful mom with her magnificent smile. It occurred to me that those pictures were there in that night table next to his/their bed because he probably still looked at them, meaning he still had a thing for my mom all these years later. As I peered deep into the fading pics, studying the outlines of their shapes, their eyes, their mouths, I began to weep for all we could have had, for all we lost. For several days I used every free moment to look at this idealized version of my parents and was grief stricken for the family I never got to have.

I showed the pictures to McDougal and his mom and direct messaged them to Jessica in Florida. I asked each of them why people couldn't stay together. Even as I asked, I knew it was a stupid, impossible question with no good answer, but I was feeling sorry for myself and was filled with righteous anger at what was taken from me. But of course, with time, a new routine, and the crush of makeup work at school, I slowly came to accept—this was just life. And the self-pity and anger morphed into more scar tissue.

Though the transition to McDougal's was hard, it kept me from dwelling on all that I'd lost. His mom took great pains to be sensitive, but still made sure I was accountable. I couldn't get used to checking in or always letting her know where I was going, so I would receive pointed texts saying for this to work, I needed to let her know where I was. She liked that I was independent about stuff like doing my laundry and making my own breakfast, and we both had fun busting McDougal's chops about being a momma's boy. At first he and I were with each other constantly, and it was a little odd since neither of us ever had any siblings, but in no time we found a good rhythm for hanging out and for giving each other space.

One thing I missed from my old life was the library. I still went, but not every night like when the old man was around. McDougal had a group Spanish project to do with some classmates and they were meeting at the library, so I went with him. One of the classmates was that girl who liked him, Olivia O'Malley.

We were the first ones there and were sitting in the magazine section near the entranceway when she came in by herself.

"I heard about your dad . . . Sorry," she told me in her pocket-sized voice.

"Thanks."

"So do you stay with an uncle or something now?"

"No," I said, nodding in McDougal's direction, "I stay with him. They're adopting me."

"Oh," she said, looking surprised.

"We're like brothers," McDougal added.

"That's odd, James. I would've thought a brother of yours

would've been shorter and whiter," she said with a deadpan smile.

I totally lost it and had to go outside I was laughing so hard. I came back in, but had to leave 'cause I started to laugh again. Mc-Dougal took this opportunity to point out what a simpleton I was, saying that I lost it like this all the time, especially when I watched my favorite TV shows, *Teen Wolf* and *Judge Judy*. It wasn't really that good of a put-down, but Olivia touched his arm and gave him a big laugh.

When the other two members of the group showed up, they went over to a corner of the library, where they worked on a short play to perform in front of their Spanish class. It was fascinating to watch Olivia—she was totally captivated by McDougal, hanging on his every word and laughing when he spoke. Walking home later, she was hilarious complaining about the lack of participation of the other two people in the group.

"They should just be props, like coat racks. We'll put our jackets over their faces. Or end tables. They'll get down on all fours and we'll put potted plants on their backs while we do the dialogue," she said in her small, energetic voice.

When we got to our turnoff, McDougal casually said, "See you at home. I'm going to show Olivia how to apply a tricky Algebra formula she missed the other day," and with a smile added, "I texted my mom."

And just like that McDougal was back in the game with some-one who was a match for him physically and intellectually. Shortly thereafter I got back in the game too. I was doing some makeup laps on the track in the auxiliary gym after school, and the six-foot-three basketball player, Jasmine Hunter, was in there practicing foul shots. I watched her go through her routine for the ten minutes I jogged around the gym and didn't see her miss one shot. Finally, just as I was finishing up, she clunked one off the back of the rim and the ball came right to me.

As I bounced it back to her, she said, "That's on you."

"Me? How's that on me?"

"You went from running to walking, and it messed with my rhythm."

"If that messed you up, how do you hit them in front of a crowd during a game?"

"It's not the volume that throws you off. It's the *change* in volume, like going from running to walking."

"Ah . . ."

"I'll demonstrate," she said. "Stand out-of-bounds behind the basket and wave your arms."

I did what she asked and she hit like five in a row. Then she told me to wave my arms and jump up and down. I did that and she hit five more. Next, I was supposed to wave my arms, jump up and down, and yell: "Miss." I did that and she hit five more.

"Okay," she said, trying not to smile. "This time wave your arms, jump up and down, do two leg kicks, and yell: 'When am I going to figure out Jasmine is totally messing with me?'"

She demonstrated, and it took a second before I got she was playing me while dying laughing, which made me laugh too.

"You would've done that all day."

"No, I would've eventually got tired and gone home," I said, still kind of laughing.

As we stood there smiling at each other, I noticed she was a little darker than me and wore her hair in a ponytail. She had bright, cheerful eyes and an athletic body. We were also about the same height and I asked her, "How tall are you?"

"Not the most original question, but I'll play along. Six-three."

"No, it's just . . . we're about the same size, and last I remember I was just six."

"Really?"

"I've kind of been through a lot lately."

"I know . . . Jackson," she said, smiling.

I got very excited she knew who I was, and from there she smoked me in a couple of one-on-one games. But she didn't just want to beat me—she wanted to practice defending and fighting through someone stronger than her on the low post. She was really competitive and at one point got mad when I half assed it, yelling at me to stand my ground or get out of the gym.

Afterward, walking home, I found out her dad was a retired Marine and she came to South Park the same year I did. We talked about the cops stopping us when we moved into the neighborhood and how upsetting it was to be stopped for no reason. After it happened a couple of times, she told her dad, who went to the station and straightened it out. When we got to her house, which was immaculate, I asked if I could call her.

"That's complicated. First, you have to call my dad and tell him you want to see me socially. Then he'll contact your parents to establish parameters."

She must have seen my eyes grow big and said, "It's not as bad as it sounds, and it's not to intimidate you. It's to make sure expectations are clear and consistent. If you don't want to that's okay, but this is the way I have to do it."

"No . . . no. I absolutely want to do it."

I called and Jasmine's mom, dad, and little sister came to Mc-

Dougal's. We had a nice little meet and greet with some drinks and coffee cake. Like Jasmine, they were big, robust people, very serious, yet totally reasonable, emphasizing how important it was to know the people their daughter was associating with in and out of school.

And just like that, Jasmine and I double-dated with McDougal and Olivia, going out to see *The Edge of Seventeen* and then to Denny's, like rich kids in the suburbs. It was a really good time, and more than that, all that stuff about mythological forces making everyone leave me seemed to vanish. This was a good place. This was where I belonged.

Near the end of November, everything was going great. We'd made it through the first hurdles of the adoption process, both of us had possible new girlfriends, and I was slowly getting my head right and was acclimating to my new situation at McDougal's house. We had a couple of unseasonably warm days, and coming home from school we noticed that the construction crew, who had been putting in new curbs all summer and fall, were packing up for the winter. McDougal complained we never got around to kicking over the parking cones on our bikes like he had seen me do with JuJu and Skeezy. Without the old man around to beat the shit out of me, I agreed to do it. So, we planned to cut out of school early the next day and give it a shot. Luckily, there were still a couple of blocks' worth of cones in place along some curbs that were still curing, which we kicked over with a vengeance like invading marauders. We got a little pushback from the construction guys, who called us "assholes" and "motherfuckers," but they didn't chase us.

We took off laughing, and down about ten blocks McDougal bombed out and needed to rest. We were right near the liquor store, and while getting his shit together he suggested we celebrate this victory by scamming a bottle, but not any shitty whiskey. Locking our bikes to a fence around the corner, we decided I would snatch a fifth of Fireball, which was some cinnamon-flavored bullshit.

And like the other times, it worked perfectly. I waited out front, saw the flicker of the lights, went in, put the Fireball in my hoodie pocket, and exited in under thirty seconds. On the way out some scruffy guy in a hoodie, moving with some fierceness, bumped me as he entered the store. I panicked momentarily as I went around the corner to our bikes, but quickly realized he would have stopped me if he were interested in the bottle I just stole.

As I worked this out, all of a sudden I heard a bunch of popping sounds. I looked around from the edge of the brick building and saw the guy who had bumped me fall back hard on the sidewalk, a gun slipping from his hand. I froze for a moment and then thought . . . *McDougal* and ran toward the store, yelling his name.

As I passed the injured guy on the ground and entered the liquor store, the old guy working the counter pointed a gun at me. I threw my hands up in the air and yelled, "No gun! . . . No gun!" Almost immediately he collapsed into a sitting position with a gaping stomach wound while I continued to call out for McDougal. I found him beneath a pile of boxes near the old man, breathing erratically, but conscious and bleeding from his chest.

"Call 911," he said, gasping for air.

Though panicked, I made the call and explained to the police dispatcher what was happening. With both shooters down, there was no immediate danger, so the dispatcher wanted to keep me on the line, but I had to help McDougal. Calmly the dispatcher told me to do that, but to put the phone on speaker and set it down.

McDougal remained awake, taking short, thin breaths, and amid all the blood, I couldn't find where he was hit and started to cry. Finally, in the upper part of his chest below his collarbone but near his heart, I found the entry spot as he winced in pain. Though tears were pouring from my eyes, I remained relatively calm, applying pressure to the wound with the heel of my hand, telling him it was all right, help was on the way, everything was going to be fine. Some guy, maybe in his twenties, came into the store yelling, "Grandpa, Grandpa," and went to the old man.

Once all the cops and ambulances arrived, I was pushed aside and became quite hysterical, thinking this was all my fault and McDougal was going to fucking die because of my stupid ass. I fucking killed everything that I touched.

Like with my old man, the cops removed me from the situation. A nice cop named Officer Russell helped clean me up and put me in a cruiser with a blanket after removing my bloody clothes. Filled with the abject dread of knowing I killed McDougal, I was still able to explain our scam and pass along McDougal's mom's number while occasionally hyperventilating.

First they put the scruffy guy, who I assumed tried to rob the liquor store, into an ambulance, then the old man, and just as they were wheeling McDougal out, his mom arrived in her work scrubs. They had him at a slight incline as she walked with him to the ambulance. She asked one of the cops something, and he pointed to the car I was sitting in with Officer Russell. As she jogged toward the cruiser in what seemed like slow motion, I braced myself for the worst possible news.

Officer Russell opened the back door for her, and she got down on her haunches and looked up at me, asking, "Are you all right?"

Through my tears all I could do was nod.

She told me James was hurt badly but was going to be all right, and she was going to ride with him in the ambulance to the hospital. The police were going to have to take me to the station for a statement and then would release me to my next of kin, which meant Teddy.

I calmed down as I waited on Teddy. However, in the intervening hours, I worked out a plan of escape. It was a bit irrational, but I was going to leave everyone before they left me. Even when I got to the hospital where McDougal's mom and dad waited, I was convinced he was going to die, despite assurances from his mom that everything was going to be all right.

So, when the surgeon came into the waiting room and said he was all buttoned up and we could see him for a moment, I braced myself for the worst. He was really groggy, and after his mom tearfully hugged him and his dad patted him on the leg between the IVs and monitors, telling him to be tough, McDougal called me over and in a whispery voice said, "This definitely is going to get me laid."

I busted out laughing and crying at the same time, realizing McDougal wouldn't be leaving anytime soon.

Epilogue

Unlike the opioid-addicted guy who tried to hold up the liquor store and in the process shot McDougal and the old dude working the counter, we had no legal consequences for the petty larceny we committed. But after McDougal was well enough, his mom made us go to both Rite Aid and the liquor store to apologize and pay for the six-packs and the bottle of Jameson we scammed. There also was a lecture about the danger we put ourselves in and how we jeopardized our futures.

On top of that, after the first of the year, McDougal was scheduled to do a semester-long Saturday-morning internship in the IT Department at the Board of Education. He was really looking forward to this opportunity, but his mom made him make an embarrassing call to his sponsor to ask if he was disqualified as a result of the poor decisions that led to him being shot in a liquor store. She made me call the social worker overseeing my adoption case and explain my shitty decisions as well. Even though he didn't lose his internship and I wasn't turned over to Child Protective Services, the message was loud and clear: both McDougal and I would be accountable. Harsh, maybe, but for the first time in my life someone cared enough to make me answer for my actions, which I really appreciated. More than that, I hated disappointing McDougal's mom.

Cleaning out the house on Lockwood, I found out that my

mom's maiden name was Boulos. I passed that information along to Jessica, and she did some digging on the internet and identified a bunch of families from my mom's town, Camp Perrin, with the same name. Of course, I wanted to dive face-first into this and was told I could if I wanted, but Jessica, McDougal's mom, and my new counselor encouraged me to move cautiously and to manage my expectations. A good course of action, they agreed, would be to continue settling into my new life and routine and really think through what contact would mean. Reluctantly, I agreed, but that didn't stop me stalking Facebook groups and walls, along with Twitter and other social media sites. I didn't find her among the endless pictures I looked at, but I had some clues and knew where I was going to check when the time was right.

It became instantly obvious making contact would create many questions of *with who, how, when, where*. And if you got through those, then you'd have to address more: *would, could, should* questions. It got so complicated, so fast, McDougal would've been hard-pressed to come up with an algorithm to deal with even the most basic obstacles. Now I got why everyone told me to move slow and to manage my expectations. Still, it was nice to think about her maybe becoming part of my life at some point, while remembering the good times from the past, like feeding the ducks at the park and going to preschool with Mr. Nate. And though the idea of contacting my mom was exciting, I was getting quite comfortable at McDougal's, liking the steady Wi-Fi, reliable meals, clean sheets, and most of all people who cared about me. I'm not sure I could endure being thrown back into the vortex of instability.

On McDougal's first day back at school just before Christmas, lots of people he didn't really know stopped him as we walked through the halls to fist-bump, high-five, and say hello. He tapped me on the shoulder and when I bent over, he again whispered in my ear, "This is so going to get me laid."

As we passed through the transition hallway to our home-rooms, rockhead McManus was there with his dumb rockhead friends. He called out to McDougal, and I clenched my fists, think-ing, *Here we go*, but he smiled his dumb rockhead smile and gave McDougal a thumbs-up. I leaned over and said, "Even McManus with the props. Maybe he could be your first conquest?"

He didn't have time to come back at me because as we exited the transition hallway, he was mauled by Lexi, who was waiting with Syd. She was both laughing and crying when she released him after an extended hug. As Syd leaned in awkwardly to hug him, Lexi looked at me and then embraced me too.

When I came back to school after the liquor store incident, a few weeks ahead of McDougal, Lexi and I finally had a real conver-sation where we both basically said the same thing: too soon, too fast, too much. Since she got in too deep with me like Groman, she vowed to steer clear of relationships for the foreseeable future, or at least until she had a better handle on how to establish and stick to boundaries. I did get to thank her for the grace she showed me when we broke up, and hopefully didn't sound like too much of a dork when I said, "There were some magic moments between us I'll always remember."

Syd was back with Gary Clausen, who did end up getting the Anthony Kiedis tattoo. Sometimes when I saw them together at lunch, I could catch her eye and would make the *L* sign up on my forehead, as in *loser*. She would smile and flip me off playfully. I was very happy our friendship got to this place.

Olivia, as it turned out, was a constant presence, much like Lexi was when we were dating. She was a pocket-sized force to be reckoned with. She and McDougal seemed to be a perfect match of size, intelligence, and ball busting. She could really get him going, telling him things like he'd be a Hufflepuff instead of a Gryffindor if we went to Hogwarts. He would get all indignant and say, "Bullshit, I got shot robbing a liquor store."

"Gryffindors are known for being brave," she would say, shaking her head. "How is doing a little magic trick with your phone and getting shot brave? And let's not be dramatic—it was only one bullet."

I really liked her and imagined this was how it would go when McDougal tried to cash in the liquor store chip. "Sex 'cause you got shot? Sorry, Hufflepuff, you're going to have to earn it."

Jasmine and I got on very well, but after a few months she dumped me too. With all that happened I was way too raw to give anything of substance to anybody, and like Lexi, she had serious plans for the future. But during our time together, we laughed and had a good time. On several occasions I participated in speed-chess tournaments at her house with friends and extended family. This was some pretty serious chess with skilled players who were also master trash-talkers. I was terrible at first and got verbally abused, to the absolute delight of everyone in attendance. I never had so much fun being so bad at anything, and as I walked home in the afterglow of one of these nights, it dawned on me why people talk about the importance of family. They talk about it and want to preserve it because it's so goddamn fun, or at least more fun than sitting in a library while your old man is getting bombed on Keystone Lights and watching goddamn Sean Hannity.

And the Hunters were so upright and classy that after Jasmine dumped me, they stopped by McDougal's and wished me well. Her mom gave me a nice hug and said it was a pleasure getting to know me, and her dad gave me a firm Marine handshake and told me to call him if I needed anything or just wanted to talk. And it was no bullshit. He looked me in the eye and I knew he meant it. If he didn't have all that rocked-up Marine shit going on, I might have hugged him and started crying.

I never got in too deep with Jasmine, so when she dumped me, it was easy to remain friends with her. On the way to class one day a few weeks after we stopped going out, she came up to me and asked if I could meet her in the auxiliary gym after school to help her with that low-post move again. "Sure," I said, but when I got there she was still in her street clothes and she dragged me into the equipment closet and started making out with me. Between kissing me and moving her hands all over my body, she said we still couldn't go out, but sometimes we could do this, if it was okay with me. I started to think through and measure out what she was asking in a serious way, but then she positioned my hands over her back pockets and kissed me again, and I just said, "Um, yeah, I can do this. This is okay."

As ironic as it might seem that I met McDougal in the *transition* hallway, it was even more ironic that a fucking U2 song had come into my head as I'd sat in the police station waiting on Teddy after he got shot. I didn't remember this until a few days later when I was a bit clearer, but that line about a shot ringing out in the Memphis sky from that song honoring Martin Luther King, "Pride (In the Name of Love)," kept repeating in my self-loathing head. Maybe worse than McDougal dying would have been remembering him with a U2 song.

This is what happens when you're not prepared—any old thing can find its way into your head and mark you for life. Except for that momentary lapse where I thought dark forces were conspiring against me, the thing I learned most since meeting McDougal, nearly a year ago, was things happen because of your actions or lack of action. Obviously, there are forces beyond your control, like having a runt with a bad Dollar Store haircut thrown at you in a hallway or having an abusive alcoholic father. You can't control that shit, but you can control how you engage or don't engage these forces, and it makes all the difference where your life goes or doesn't go.

I'm pretty sure at some point, when my life is more stable and pointed in a direction of my making, I'm going to contact my mom. Hopefully, it will be a joyous meeting, but whatever happens I'll be prepared with proper expectations. In the meantime, I'm going to gather my power and try to get ahead of some shit. Like the next time McDougal's life is in danger or if he gets shot again, so I don't have some goddamn U2 anthem just popping into my head, I've decided I'm going to think of him in terms of this short, high-energy, existential banger called "Captain's Dead" by Guided by Voices. It'll be a nice tribute to the person he was while being appropriate for slam dancing.

Getting ahead of shit and taking action—it makes all the difference in the coming and going, leaving and not leaving.

Acknowledgments

Great thanks to my wonderful family: Donna. Madeline Caroline and Patrick for putting up with me through the production of this book. Supportive and dismissive in equal measure you are a constant source of joy. Additional thanks to the fabulous Caroline Kane for her stunning artwork. See more of her work at carolinekane.net

I would also like express my gratitude to beta readers: Steve Sorra, Dave Smith, Tim Watts and Mary Lou Nolan. Your thoughtful criticism and encouragement made this a much better book.

Thanks to Nancy Bizup, Ned Kennedy and Rosemary Southwick for helping to make scenes and characters authentic with your expert consultation.

A final thanks to editor Nikki Mentges of NAM Editorial for the endless help fixing my dangling modifiers, comma splices and for shaping this book into a coherent, grammatically correct work. (She's cringing right now at that last sentence's lack of parallel structure).

About the Author...

P.A. Kane lives in West Seneca, N.Y. with his wife Donna and their three college age children. He is the author of "Written In The Stars: The Book Of Molly," and is the publisher of the satire site Buffalomud.com. For all things P.A. Kane check his website: www.pakane.net and his Amazon author page. You can also find him on Facebook and Twitter.